# COMMON PEOPLE

PHILIP CALLOW was born at Stechford, Birmingham in 1924 to a working-class family. In a career spanning almost fifty years, Callow published poetry, sixteen volumes of fiction, and several biographies, including works on D. H. Lawrence, Van Gogh, Whitman, Cézanne, and Chekhov. His novels include his highly acclaimed debut *The Hosanna Man* (1956), which was withdrawn and pulped in response to a threatened libel suit; *Common People* (1958), which critic John Betjeman hailed as one of the best books of the year; and a trilogy of autobiographical novels often regarded as his finest work: *Going to the Moon* (1968), *The Bliss Body* (1969), and *Flesh of Morning* (1971). Callow died in 2007.

BEN CLARKE is Associate Professor of Twentieth-Century British Literature at University of North Carolina at Greensboro. He is the author of *Orwell in Context: Communities, Myths, Values* (Palgrave, 2007), and co-author, with Michael Bailey and John K. Walton, of *Understanding Richard Hoggart: A Pedagogy of Hope* (Wiley-Blackwell, 2011).

Philip Callow

# COMMON PEOPLE

WITH A NEW INTRODUCTION BY
**BEN CLARKE**

VALANCOURT BOOKS

# INTRODUCTION

When *Common People* was first published in 1958, John Betjeman described it as "a genuine cry from a class usually silent in the literary world."[1] The novel seemed to exemplify a shift, not only in the subject matter of literature but the kinds of people who produced it. *Common People* appeared in the same year as Alan Sillitoe's *Saturday Night and Sunday Morning*, Shelagh Delaney's *A Taste of Honey*, and Arnold Wesker's *Chicken Soup with Barley*, and only shortly after John Osborne's *Look Back in Anger* (1956) and John Braine's *Room at the Top* (1957). These texts all contributed to what David Lodge described as the "displacement of a literary establishment that was constituted of ageing remnants of pre-war modernism, Bloomsbury, and bohemianism, that was predominantly middle to upper-middle class, public-school and Oxbridge-educated, domiciled in central London or the country ... by a new generation of writers who were working class or lower-middle class in social background" and who wrote about "places largely neglected by the most prestigious writers of the 1940s – northern industrial towns, dull suburbs, provincial universities".[2] As Julian Symons argued in a review of Callow's first novel *The Hosanna Man* (1956), "Britain's literary Bohemia" had "shifted since the war from London to the provinces".[3] Some of the most challenging and exciting literature of the period was produced by those outside what Jack Common called the "writing classes,"[4] by young men and women from "Leeds and

[1] C. Atlee et al., "Books of the Year – I: Chosen by Eminent Contemporaries," *The Sunday Times*, December 21, 1958, p. 6.

[2] D. Lodge, "Richard Hoggart: A Personal Appreciation," in Sue Owen, ed., *Re-reading Richard Hoggart: Life, Literature, Language, Education* (Newcastle: Cambridge Scholars, 2008), 1-10, p. 3.

[3] J. Symons, "Scraping a Living," *Times Literary Supplement*, April 6, 1956, p. 205.

[4] J. Common, "Preface," in Jack Common, ed., *Seven Shifts* (1938; repr. Wakefield, E. P. Publishing, 1978), vii-xi, p. vii.

Manchester, Birmingham and Swansea,"[1] who had their own convictions and concerns, distinct from those of their metropolitan predecessors.

Philip Callow seemed to typify this new generation of artists. He was born in 1924 in Stechford, Birmingham, and grew up in what he later described as "a tidy, law-abiding slum".[2] His father was an upholsterer and clerk, and Callow himself worked as a lathe apprentice after leaving technical college. When *The Hosanna Man* was published he was working for the South West Electricity Board, where he remained for a further ten years. His work explores the experience of provincial artists and intellectuals and was praised by contemporary reviewers for its sensitive portrayals of working-class life. Penelope Mortimer argued that "the first forty pages of ... 'Common People,' are the most brilliantly successful account of English working-class life I have ever encountered in any medium",[3] and Richard Mayne insisted that "Philip Callow and Alan Sillitoe ... document working-class life far more authentically than their predecessors, and the patrons of their predecessors, in the thirties."[4] Articulate, skeptical of authority, and frustrated by the drabness and constraints of post-war English life, Callow might easily be seen as one of the "angry young men" whose image dominated much discussion of cultural change in the late nineteen-fifties, but the term simplifies his achievement even as it locates him within twentieth-century literary history.

The label "angry young men" was contested almost as soon as it was coined. In his introduction to *Declaration*, Tom Maschler condemned the ways in which it had been "employed to group, without so much as an attempt at understanding, all those sharing a certain indignation against the apathy, the complacency, the idealistic bankruptcy of their environment." He recognized

[1] J. Symons, "Scraping a Living," *Times Literary Supplement*, April 6, 1956, p. 205.
[2] P. Callow, *Passage from Home: A Memoir* (Nottingham: Shoestring Press, 2002), p. 2.
[3] P. Mortimer, "A White Hope?" *The Sunday Times*, August 10, 1958, p. 7.
[4] R. Mayne, "Tendencies in the Year's Fiction," *The Sunday Times*, December 28, 1958, p. 10.

that many writers had "set themselves the task of waking us up,"[1] but emphasized their diversity, the fact that they "do not belong to a united movement."[2] Describing Callow as an angry young man emphasizes the historical context of his work but obscures the distinct qualities of his response to post-war British life. Even some contemporary reviewers recognized that his work could not simply be equated with that of contemporaries such as John Osborne, Kingsley Amis and John Wain. Arthur Calder-Marshall argued that Callow "avoided the brashness of an angry young man"[3] in *Common People* and Isabel Quigly emphasized the originality of the novel, which "would seem to have no likely followers and no direct antecedents," and offered "the voice of ... an individual, speaking from the heart about things of human importance".[4]

*Common People* is not only characterized by its individual narrative voice but its insistent concern with individuality. It explores this largely through the struggles of its protagonist, Nick Chapman, who is torn between his desire to belong and fear of being trapped. His flight to London is a response to feeling "cramped"[5] in Woodfield and his need to escape the factory work that "had begun to crush and hammer me into a tool like all the others."[6] He hopes to break "free of the past" and establish the conditions for "a new life"[7] in the capital, to realize the "secret part of myself" that wants "to be a poet, or an artist of some kind".[8] This fantasy of escape is shared by his lover Jessie Hammond, who longs "to get away" from Birmingham, which she finds "mean and small".[9] In the end, both are driven back to the Midlands as a consequence of Nick's need "to be married and to know common joys," his

[1] T. Maschler, "Introduction," *Declaration* (1957; repr. New York: E.P. Dutton, 1958), 7-9, p. 7.

[2] Ibid., p. 8.

[3] A. Calder-Marshall, "Light and Shade," *Times Literary Supplement*, August 29, 1958, p. 481.

[4] I. Quigly, "Novels," *Encounter*, November 1958, p. 84.

[5] Callow, *Common People*, p. 61.

[6] Ibid., p. 63.

[7] Ibid., p. 64.

[8] Ibid., p. 32.

[9] Ibid., p. 105.

conviction that until he does so he is "only waiting, marking time, wasting my life."[1] Although he recognizes that Jessie is "afraid of exposing herself to more injury" after her divorce, he cannot accept her argument that they are "better ... as lovers,"[2] and needs the socially-recognized stability of marriage. When he returns to see his parents in Woodfield at Christmas, "married, and therefore a potential family man," he feels his "days of anger and revolt were done with,"[3] and by the end of the text he has a son and a job in an insurance office. He has seemingly been restored to the common people, to the conventional structures and values against which he briefly rebels.

John Rodden and John Rossi describe Gordon Comstock, the protagonist of George Orwell's *Keep the Aspidistra Flying*, as an "'Angry Young Man' of the 1930s,"[4] but the differences between the conclusion of Orwell's novel and that of *Common People* are revealing. In *Keep the Aspidistra Flying*, Rosemary's pregnancy brings to an end Gordon's rebellion against the "money-god,"[5] restoring him to "decent, fully human life."[6] In *Common People*, Nick senses the "wind of spring"[7] after the birth of his son but is not securely reintegrated in the world he rejected. His "days of ... revolt" are contained rather than concluded and his dissatisfaction finds expression in both his persistent desire to "[p]aint ... [w]rite poetry"[8] and his concern with outcasts, those who lack a stable social position or function. Even before he leaves for London he is fascinated by the old man "who stalked about Woodfield with long, slow strides, majestic as an Egyptian king,"[9] and at the end of the text Jessie recognizes that his memories of an "old vagrant

---

[1] Ibid., p. 116.

[2] Ibid., p. 134.

[3] Ibid., p. 137.

[4] J. Rodden and John Rossi, *The Cambridge Introduction to George Orwell* (Cambridge: Cambridge University Press, 2012), p. 88

[5] G. Orwell, *Keep the Aspidistra Flying* (1936; repr. Harmondsworth: Penguin, 1989), p. 267.

[6] Ibid., p. 265.

[7] Callow, *Common People*, p. 161.

[8] Ibid., p. 154.

[9] Ibid., p. 22.

I had tried to sketch in the Deptford café"[1] are bound up with his "itch to wander," his belief that "[t]here's a vagabond ... in every man somewhere."[2] Nick has chosen "common joys," but his attempt to achieve a "fully human life" is an ongoing struggle to reconcile his sense of himself with his need for others.

The challenge of expressing individuality within general structures is apparent in Nick's relation to language. As Terry Eagleton argues, the "meaning of language is a social matter: there is a real sense in which language belongs to my society before it belongs to me".[3] It is precisely this quality that Nick distrusts, as he fears his distinct experiences will be lost in a common system. Words appear to him "a snare, a quagmire, a deadly trap,"[4] and he argues to Jessie that "[w]e'd be saner without tongues – and much happier, too."[5] Nick cannot reject language, but is cautious of it, refusing to take it for granted, to accept its ready-made forms and their easy consolations. A similar productive skepticism is apparent in Callow himself, whose striking eloquence is partly a result of his economy and determined rejection of cliché. Nick finds the poems written by Lanyon, a fellow factory worker, "stilted, corpse-like things, encrusted with wordy metaphors," and can dispel his distaste only by returning his attention to "the lathe and the cast-iron."[6] Callow similarly uses a close attention to the ordinary and concrete to oppose the dead forms he inherited. The result, Isabel Quigly argues, is a style "so direct it scarcely has the form of fiction, so present it is painful, so truthful it is cleansing, salutary, and exhilarating."[7]

There is plenty of anger in *Common People*, anger at the needless ugliness of modern cities, at the alienating, repetitive forms of industrial labour and, above all, at the social structures and conventions that prevent people from fulfilling themselves. Existing conditions not only constrain the lives of an artistic minority,

[1] Ibid., p. 155.
[2] Ibid., p. 156.
[3] T. Eagleton, *Literary Theory: An Introduction* (1983; repr. Oxford: Blackwell, 1995), p. 71.
[4] Callow, *Common People*, p. 33.
[5] Ibid., p. 113.
[6] Ibid., p. 43.
[7] Quigly, "Novels," p. 84.

such as the "different and irresponsible"[1] amateur painter Cecil Luce, but people like Nick's father, a "shy man" with "the northerner's distrust of words,"[2] and his mother, "eternally chained"[3] to her kitchen. Growing up on a "nondescript and ugly"[4] street, Nick cannot even "imagine a future, which ... brought change and opportunity."[5] Anger alone cannot explain so complex and subtle a novel, though, just as it cannot explain Callow himself. The significance and value of *Common People* derives in part from its sensitivity to the contradictory forces that act upon its characters. Nick feels "affection"[6] for the place he flees, and is tormented by a need "for contact, for real friendship"[7] even as he seeks out solitude. The novel refuses simple solutions, arguing that these tensions between anger and desire cannot be finally resolved by painting, returning home, marriage or even the birth of a child but must be constantly renegotiated. In contrast to much preceding literary fiction, which represented emotional and moral complexity as the prerogative of an artistic and social minority, it is alert to the struggles and value of the supposedly ordinary lives played out in provincial towns, in factories and insurance offices. The result is not only anger at the structures that constrain such lives, but an insistence that, as Raymond Williams insisted, "there are in fact no masses, but only ways of seeing people as masses."[8] The neglect of this intelligent, sophisticated, often lyrical novel is one more indication that this argument needs to be made again.

BEN CLARKE

---

[1] Callow, *Common People*, p. 46.
[2] Ibid., p. 137.
[3] Ibid., p. 16.
[4] Ibid., p. 15.
[5] Ibid., p. 9.
[6] Ibid., p. 15.
[7] Ibid., p. 34.
[8] R. Williams, "Culture is Ordinary" in Robin Gable, ed., *Resources of Hope: Culture, Democracy, Socialism* (London: Verso, 1989), 3-18, p. 11.

# One

## i

I remember my grandfather. If I look back at my early life, trying to recall it, the old man comes first to my mind. He rises up immediately, before anything else—I suppose because he made the most vivid impression. I remember him now as something solid and enduring: more permanent than the house we all lived in, which was badly in need of attention, and had the germ of its end lodged almost visibly in the fissures and rotten wood and walls trying to shed their plaster. Compared to it he seemed ageless. I cannot think what the house was like without him, yet in fact he did not come to live with us as one of the family until after the death of my grandmother.

When she died, the love in my world seemed to diminish. It happened just after I changed from one school to another, so I must have been eleven. It was a sudden death, and my mother said afterwards that there was no reason for it, no cause. She had not been ill. It was simply that she was very tired and wanted to rest: so she stopped. And I remember that my father cried in my presence for the first and only time, bowing his head suddenly and hiding his face. I thought he had a headache, or felt suddenly weary; he often did that, rubbing his face and shutting the light from his eyes because they ached. But with a slow horror rising in me I heard a faint choking sound from behind his hands.

"Your father's upset," my mother said. "I should come in here a minute."

I left the room and stood in the kitchen, confused and ashamed, crushed and terrified by this sudden calamity. Then after a few minutes everything returned to normal. I went back and sat staring into the fire, afraid to look at my father. When I finally did so I was astonished to see no sign, no change in his face. Of course I did not understand what death was, but I knew that something dark and unalterable had happened, covering the top of the street like a black slate, and it shocked me to see how quickly it was whipped away.

My grandmother was a busy, fluttering woman, always working. She had a wonderful, tender smile, a smile of such sweetness that I can see it now as vividly as ever. It struck root in my memory, a secret root of joy in my childhood, and now it blossoms forth, a tender foliage. Her soft cries of delight, her vigorous laughter, ring in my ears again.

"Bless him, then," she would cry, bent over some task in the wooden kitchen, as she caught sight of me peering in at her through the door. "Why, hallo, my love! Well I never, well I never! Have you come to see poor old Granny? Come here, come to me, sweetheart!"

Her hands fluttered like birds with excitement. And she would gather me in her arms, pressing me to her strongly, with such a fierce and tender joy, that I was infused and almost overwhelmed by her love, like a small tree overladen with fruit. It was as if the young gave her such delight that she became young again herself, transformed by her own happiness. All the burden of her hard life seemed to fall away, and though her back stooped she had no longer seemed old. Her silky white hair was a mistake then. Her crippled swollen hands, smelling of flour, were as gentle as a girl's as they stroked my cheeks and hair.

She lived on the outskirts of the city, in a bungalow made by nailing grey asbestos sheets to a wooden frame, which had been built by my grandfather and one of his workmates at the end of the First World War. It was erected on a largish plot of land, and used to be almost on its own in the country. Then the city crept up to it, and the bungalow itself was slowly surrounded, until it stood in the midst of a colony of squalid wooden shacks. Eventually this colony grew into a disgraceful collection of about fifty dwellings called Woodland Gardens, and it had dirt lanes running through it, which I explored as though I wandered in a strange land, fascinated by the difference between them and the city streets I lived in. I looked on it all as an exotic, exciting country, like a shanty town I had read about, a place in Jamaica.

The bungalow possessed a wooden veranda, running the

whole length of one side. On my visits there I paced along it and gazed out over the tin roofs and distant factories, engaged in fantastic solitary adventures. What more could a boy want than a veranda! Sometimes, on hot summer days, I would be on a Mexican ranch, and the aluminium ventilators on the squat roofs of workshops became the peaks of glittering mountains. If I knelt down, peering through the wooden slats, I could see water glinting below, in the storage tank, and farther back a big heap of coal ready for the winter, and maybe the glowing green eyes, like stars, of a cat in the shade.

Occasionally I was allowed to stay the night, or even for a whole fortnight during my holidays in August. The garden gate squealed on its rusty hinges when I pushed it open, and the spaniel bitch came racing to meet me, delirious with joy. This dog, Blackface, was an amazingly gentle creature, following me everywhere, waiting outside my bedroom for me to get up. As I lay on the lawn, which seemed to be flapping under my back like a great hairy flag when the wind blew, Blackface would come and lick at the roots of my hair. I would absorb the sun, hour after hour, on those hot August days, until I staggered on my legs like a bee.

The mornings especially were a magical time. I lay very still, listening to the two sons going off to work; or, if I woke early enough, the light just beginning to filter through the yellow blind, I could hear the first morning sounds, which always made me hold my breath and listen harder, wondering if I was mistaken. Then more definite sounds would break the deep silence: a creaking door, the curtains in the living-room letting out a screech as they were drawn apart, the sounds of my grandmother starting work all over again. Then the odour of paraffin would reach me, and gradually the delicious breakfast smells, so that when she came to wake me I was ready to spring out.

"God bless you, you're awake!" she cried, bending over to touch my face. "Up you get, then, I've laid the table. Are you hungry, my love?"

In the living-room that looked on to the veranda, I sat watching the fire, the flames coming up through the round hole in the top of the black iron range, where the cooking was done. The odour of breakfast was everywhere. From my place at the table against the window I could survey the whole scene, often so luminous and glittering with dew and sunlight that I could hardly wait to finish the meal. The apple trees against the hedge spread their black crooked branches over the five hens; and that mysterious corner at the bottom, where there was a large cess-pit filled to the brim with stagnant green water, covered with slimy boards, had two fat frogs always in residence. I was going to poke one with a stick to make it move, if it was still sitting there, with its huge pop-eyes and swelling throat.

During the evenings, if either of her sons spoke roughly to her, complainingly, my grandmother would blush and grow agitated. Then she redoubled her efforts to please, to remedy the fault, whatever it was—perhaps only a cup of tea she had forgotten to sugar. Somebody would shout, "Ugh! What's this supposed to be, Mother?" And if they teased her she would hang her head and laugh softly, like a shy girl, crying: "Go on with you! Oh, you are a fool, our Fred!" And I would sit there uneasily, sharing her bashfulness.

I remember waking up in the middle of one night, terrified by some vague disaster that loomed up monstrously all around me in the unfamiliar room. I think I had dreamed of a fire burning down my home and killing my mother. I sat upright in the swirling darkness, gripped by this nightmare, and my grandmother came rushing in to console me. She was like an apparition. Her soft white hair hung loose, and there was a vast amount of it, flowing down to her waist in long waves. I was amazed, and shocked because I hardly knew her. In the midst of that mass of hair her face seemed lost, shrunken. But her gentle words and hands soon comforted me; before she left the room the strange rush of grief had gone, and I lay quiet and still, fascinated by this transfiguration, gazing in wonder at her head and nightgown.

ii

Sometimes my grandfather was there, during my visits, but more often he was away, or just about to depart. His job as a guard on the railway kept him away for two or three days at a time, according to his shift.

In the dark corridor of the bungalow which led to bedrooms, there hung a large Victorian print, depicting one of the great London stations. I used to glance at it on the way to bed. The vast, arched cavern, smoke-filled, swarming with tiny black figures, could have illustrated Dante. It frightened me vaguely, though it was quite a luxurious fear, like looking into the mouth of hell from a safe place. For all I knew, as I gazed at it from my solid haven, it might not even have existed in reality. Certainly I never dreamed of connecting it with my grandfather.

For nearly thirty years he had been a railwayman, first of all in the goods yard, then engaged on repair work, working up and down the tracks from a line-keeper's hut. Then he was promoted to a guard, eight years before the end of his service.

The new uniform made him childishly proud. He was continually stooping to knock specks of dust from his shiny trousers. He never forgot the red braid, resplendent above the peak of his cap, that caught the sun, and the word 'Guard' in red letters on the dark lapels of his jacket. Best of all, perhaps, was the scarlet piping which ran down the length of his trousers. It leapt out of his pockets and ran down the seams. He brushed that daily with a little stiff brush to keep it bright.

When he came off duty, swinging a square attaché case, he went down his rows of gooseberry bushes as if he were inspecting a line of wagons. Being a short man he was inclined to strut whenever he felt important. If I watched him coming off duty, he strutted, and if he snapped his fingers with a loud dry sound as he advanced, I knew he was pleased about something.

He always stopped walking, wherever he was, to consult the heavy watch in his waistcoat, sliding it out with a smooth turn on to his hand, slow and deliberate, his elbows protruding like the stumps of wings. He announced the exact time, in minutes and seconds, as the watch slid back and vanished with the same oiled motion.

Once or twice, in the room with him, I heard him grunt and lean closer to the window, squinting out over the lawn towards his apple trees.

"What is it?" my grandmother said, her hands twitching with irritation. "What can you see now?"

He hardly ever answered. My grandmother glared at his head and tried to contain herself, while he squinted out obstinately.

One day I heard him mutter under his breath: "There's somebody down there."

My grandmother heard. She slipped in like a wasp, quick with annoyance.

"Where?" she cried. "Whereabouts?"

"By my apples."

He had spoken without moving his head, staring out.

"Oh, heavens!" my grandmother exclaimed, and turned to her son, Fred. "Look at him again—going silly in the head! He thinks somebody's stealing his apples!"

Her son only shrugged and went on reading his newspaper.

"I saw somebody," the old man muttered.

"You saw somebody? You and your apples. Why don't you count them?"

"He does," the son said, behind his paper.

My grandmother kept glaring at him, in exasperation or contempt, but he would not leave the window.

"Look at the guard," she mocked.

She made a clicking noise with her tongue. Nothing annoyed her more than these mysterious trespassings that no one but the old man ever saw. He was getting deaf, though nobody knew how deaf he really was. It may have been a defence, so that he could ignore my grandmother's attacks and sit in peace, silent as smoke, watching for strangers in his garden.

iii

He had only been retired two years when my grandmother died. He was left alone. Fred, the oldest unmarried son, had gone in the Army. The other one, Alan, was lodging at Wolverhampton, where he was a garage mechanic. There was a married daughter who lived in Yorkshire, and my father. So my grandfather came to live with us, bringing one or two possessions. Everything else, including the bungalow, was put up for sale.

We lived on the other side of the city, at Woodfield, a small town which had quickly become part of Birmingham, though it still kept its own market, its own shopping centre, and was regarded by the older ones as a town in its own right. There was a local paper, which fostered a sort of local patriotism, keeping its own gossip alive in the very teeth of the city. But it was like living in the shadow of a giant. In a few years' time the busy sprawling giant would notice this part it had overlooked, and obliterate its individuality. Everyone knew it was inevitable.

It was a period when work was scarce, and my father, who was an upholsterer by trade, had been on short time for the last six months. So my grandfather could only have been an extra burden to us. True, he received a pension, and a superannuation from the railway. But that was a mere pittance.

Everything that was put before him he ate. His health was excellent. Even so, his appetite was amazing for such a small man.

Now our family had increased to five. My sister Irene, who was still a baby, slept in the same room as my mother and father. I shared the remaining bedroom with my grandfather. I had a narrow camp-bed near the window, against the matchboard partition which hid the stairs, and in the centre of the room stood a huge brass bedstead. Perhaps it was not huge, but it swallowed nearly all the small space. This ancient sleeping apparatus was my grandfather's property. It looked like a derelict steam-engine.

I used to lie in the darkness waiting for him to come up. He climbed the stairs each night at the stroke of eleven, after winding up the big pendulum clock, which also belonged to him, and hung now in the living-room, above the table. Once in the bedroom his routine never varied. He dragged off his trousers and long woollen underpants, then fell on his knees to say his prayers. He collapsed suddenly, all in a heap, letting out a tremendous gasp, and knelt there in silence like a motionless camel. Sometimes he combined two operations, scratching his hairy legs and praying simultaneously. Or if it were a bitterly cold night he would pass water too, getting everything cleared up in one speedy performance. I used to watch him in fascination from between the sheets. He had a short, shaggy body. Finally he stood erect for one last vigorous bout of scratching, thrusting his arms under his shirt. Then he toppled over sideways, like a felled tree, and immediately the bed gave a great rusty squeal of pain.

It was more a hammock than a bed. The broken springs had been mended with string so often that a dark ominous bulge appeared underneath, almost scraping the floor. In a matter of seconds he was unconscious, and after a few minutes his wild snoring gushed out and filled the room.

I remember vividly one night of terror in that room. A few doors along the street there was a butcher's shop, and in two rooms above it lived a couple with three children. They could only reach their rooms by the back way, down the entry behind our house, but I never once saw them. In the yard behind the shop was a broken corrugated-iron shed, where this couple used to keep their pram. The shed belonged to the butcher; it was stacked with sides of meat and hung with carcasses. The back entry where I played with friends became filled with a sickening smell if the wind blew in our direction. There were chunks of fat and gristle scattered about in the dirt of the yard, which even the dogs had left. I could not believe that a family lived there, over that repulsive place, wrapped about in that terrible rancid stench.

One night I woke up in fear. I was trembling. The old man snored peacefully, floating on the swell of his own sound. I could hear battering, splintering sounds, like furniture being violently smashed, and a woman screaming without a break. Doors opened, voices shouted questions. Somebody yelled: "Hey! What's the bloody game?" A voice I recognised cried: "Fetch the police!" Then the battering and screaming began again. And then an awful silence, full of terror and ugliness, broken by a baby's cries. When that ceased I could hear a hubbub of excited conversation and shocked whispering, underneath the bedroom window somewhere. I lay listening for at least an hour, unable to stop shivering. Pity and horror kept clawing at me, until I fell asleep.

The next day I learnt from scraps of talk that the man had arrived home drunk, and began smashing things and beating his wife.

But somehow it did not satisfy me, this explanation. The terror of the night seemed to concern everybody, to implicate them all, even my mother and father. What did it mean? It was embedded in so many things; the darkness, the corrugated-iron shed, the foul stench, the silence, the lumps of fat covered in dirt, and the gnawing mystery of the nameless couple I had not seen. I felt for the first time that I was a member of the human family, and so implicated with the others.

For days afterwards I searched the faces confronting me in the streets, the faces of my parents, for some sign, some explanation which would make all things clear: a reassurance. I felt certain that the violence had registered, and not been lost, and I expected to stumble on its traces suddenly, find it written distinctly in words I would understand at once. At night I still heard the screams, as I lay there, pondering, in the vast silence lapping against the stars.

It troubled me for a week. Then it dropped away and was forgotten, and other things pressed forward to replace it.

I committed my most secret tears to the pillow of that narrow stretcher-bed. On Sunday nights, with school looming up black and inevitable in the darkness, I used to mutter, "Don't come, Monday! Don't come, Monday!" with an intense and savage misery. I hated that school. The realisation that I had been happy at the previous one made it even more bitter. I prayed that the teachers might die, that the building would burn down, that floods or snowstorms would make the journey impossible—anything to ward off Monday morning. I cannot recall now what it was that I found so harrowing, as I cycled across the city, the machine carrying me forward at a horrifying speed. I think it was connected in some way with the cinema hoardings I passed. Perhaps it was because, on Friday afternoons, speeding home gratefully, I noticed the announcements of the films for the following week, and on these black Mondays I found myself faced with the same posters. They must have pierced me with my past happiness. Being a child, I could not imagine a future, which moved up to you and brought change and opportunity. That ray of hope is denied a child. My childhood stretched on and on. If I wished for anything it was to be an old man like my grandfather, going deaf and pottering about the house and street, with nothing to worry him.

iv

Yet he had troubles of his own, though of course I attached no importance to them. He was a diabetic. I discovered this quickly enough, because when he came to live with us it was my mother who had to give him the insulin injections. It was a daily task. She stood ready with a wad of cotton wool dabbed in methylated spirits. She would hold the syringe and little phial up to the light, filling the instrument as the doctor had shown her, while the old man rolled back his sleeve reluctantly.

"Careful now, you cruel cat," he always said.

"Keep still, then. Don't shout till you're hurt. There! How's that?"

She held the loose flesh of the arm between her thumb and finger, and dabbed at the wound. "That all right?" she shouted.

"Ugh! Like a nail!" he would groan, sucking in his breath, pulling his sleeve down gingerly over the sore place.

Once, the needle broke off in his arm, and the whole household was thrown into an uproar. He had taken off his shoes and socks, as he always did, before going to bed. He roared like an enraged bull and danced about on the stone flags of the kitchen with bare feet. They rushed him off to the hospital to have the needle removed. Upstairs my sister sobbed with fright.

Later, acting on fresh instructions from the doctor, my mother injected smaller doses into his arm, twice a day. But at the beginning of this new procedure there was some new confusion about the amount, and he received too little. It was a Sunday afternoon, so he lay resting upstairs. Suddenly a commotion started up over our heads, and my mother went pale.

"Quickly! He's having a fit!" she cried, and my father leapt to his feet automatically.

"What is it?" he said, bewildered, still clutching his Sunday paper. "Where?"

"Oh be quick!" my mother cried. "He'll bite his tongue!"

And my father scrambled up the steep stairs to hold the old man on the bed and put something between his teeth.

We had been waiting less than five minutes when he came down again. He was breathing heavily, and looked pale with exhaustion.

"Is he all right?" my mother whispered.

He nodded, standing limply, with loose hands.

"Come and sit down," she said, full of concern, "and I'll make some tea. What happened?"

"He's asleep," my father said, sinking into a chair. "It took me all my time to hold the old devil. He's as strong as a horse."

"Good heavens!" my mother exclaimed. She seemed really impressed, putting awe and respect into her voice, as she bustled into the kitchen and back. Then she asked: "Is he asleep now?"

My father wrinkled his face, looking at me for sympathy. "I just told you," he said. He drew a deep breath. "And for God's sake, woman—watch that insulin!"

v

A strange relationship existed between the two men, although they were father and son. Even physically they were very different. Grandfather was small, stocky, and my father was a tall, lean man, long in the leg, with a high bush of wiry black hair making him look even taller. His blue eyes, clean-shaven face and slightly protruding teeth gave him an appearance all his own, with no hint of my grandfather in it. It was hard to believe that they were related, glancing at them both. You had to look closely, and notice a similar dark pigmentation around the eyes. That was the only likeness. But there was a silent disapproval lurking behind my father's attitude, and an indulgence in my grandfather's, which bound them together. It was strange, though perhaps not uncommon. I think the old man was a little jealous of his son, as if he did not enjoy being displaced as the head of the household.

My father, for his part, took an off-hand, almost contemptuous attitude towards the old man—probably because he was younger in ideas as well as years. Or was it simply that the old man had been tyrannical and heavy-handed in the past, as I heard them say, and now my father's time had come? At any rate, my grandfather reacted to all this in an effective, sly manner, expressing his feelings about it, and about his new status, by calling his son 'boss'. It may have been mockery. There seemed something sardonic in the set of his head as he said it—though I believe he was really content to let somebody else be in authority now, over his head, shouldering all the responsibility. Like most old men he was selfish. He only wanted to be left in peace. He was almost completely deaf now, or so we thought. Nobody was quite sure.

"He's not as deaf as all that," my father would say. "He hears what he wants. You don't find him last getting to the table." And he always added darkly: "I wouldn't say too much in front of him."

I used to comb his hair sometimes, because my mother said he was too lazy to do it himself. His hair was thin, but still as black as my father's. The scurf dropped down on his shoulders. He sat in his leather armchair, reading one of his thrillers, while I leaned over him, trying to create a straight parting. Then he stood up, and my mother fixed his collar, scolding him because it was such a disgrace. Finally she turned to me, as I knew she would.

"Nicky, fetch the scissors."

This was to trim his greying moustache, and then his eyebrows, and the coarse tufts sprouting from his ears and nostrils. At last he was ready.

"Where are you going?" my mother shouted. He watched her mouth, though he must have known what she would ask.

"Up the town," he said loudly, if it was Saturday night. And I would set off with him, striding out gladly.

He loved to trail around the shops and market endlessly, looking for bargains. And his idea of a bargain was something big for a small price, regardless of quality. His eyes fastened on size and quantity, the bigger the better.

"More junk," my father muttered each time. "Look at it—piles of rubbish! I suppose he paid thruppence for the lot, so he thinks it's a bargain."

But the old man dived out again, on another expedition. He came home in triumph occasionally with carrier bags splitting with their loads of cheap vegetables, from stalls which were just closing down.

"Here!" he said in triumph, to my mother.

Often, when I was with him, friends would stop him and shout news in his ear, making me blush with embarrassment if we were in a crowded street.

"Hello, Bert!" they shouted, "Bert Chapman!" And he jerked round, wide-eyed, then hung his head and waited, as they tried to talk to him. It always seemed strange, hearing his name shouted aloud.

On these nights he was like a dynamo. He would bring me back so that I could go off to bed, then rush out again. He seemed tireless.

"Where does he get the energy from?" my mother said, astonished.

But my father shook his head in disgust.

One Saturday night in December found me in tears, because I was not allowed to go out with him a second time, through the exciting Christmas blaze of shops and full narrow streets. I pleaded that it was a special occasion, and thought hungrily of the acetylene flares blowing and hissing on the stall corners in the sharp air, vibrating on their brackets, and the dense throngs treading in mud and trampled garbage, through the night market.

My father stood up menacingly.

"Go to bed," he ordered. "You heard your mother."

I went to the stairs door. The stairs were hidden from the living-room by a wooden partition, as in my bedroom. It made one wall of the room. In a mad fit of rebellion I banged on it furiously as I clambered up, weeping, using my fists like hammers.

"No! No! No! No!" I yelled through my tears, and gave one last thump on the boards.

There was a loud crash. I put my eye to a crack in the boards to look down into the living-room, and was terrified by what I saw. My grandfather's large clock, which had hung on the partition, was lying on the table beneath, smashed to pieces. One of my blows must have dislodged it.

Without being able to move I saw my father jump up in a fury, staring round wildly for something to snatch up, so that he could give me a thrashing. My mother was trying to pull him back, begging him to wait, and the old man sat where he was, twisted round in his armchair, looking. Probably he had not heard the crash, but his face wore a startled expression as he looked at the wreckage of his clock. It was not angry, his face; only mildly astonished.

Then he spoke.

"Don't hit him, boss," he said. "It don't matter."

I fled, after hearing that, and locked the bedroom door. I lay waiting, gripping the sheets. Nobody came up. After about half an hour I crept out and unlocked the door. Much later, my mother brought me some supper, whispering that she was glad to see the end of that clock. It was ugly as sin, she said. She touched my head before she left, and I cheered up a little, and felt less like a criminal, and the bones began to come back in my body.

# Two

i

Our street was nondescript and ugly. Two identical rows of brick terraces faced each other, forty-six houses long, with thin slits cutting through, which were the entries of cindery dirt, puddled with bits of sky and jewelled with spittle, leading to all the back places. The front doors opened on to the pavement. Very gradually I came to realise how hideous the street was. Meanwhile, I had an affection for it. I knew every doorstep.

There was something strange about one of the houses. Its two street windows were blind, sealed up with sore, orange bricks. Behind there lived the terribly thin woman who brought round our firewood. Her clothes flapped on her body. She never washed. Her face was black like a charred root, and as she passed by on the pavement she turned her scorching hot gaze on you. Nobody was surprised one April when she was taken away raving mad.

At one end of the street stood the local cinema, the Acropolis. It always looked bright and impudent with new paint, dripping blobs of red and gold light on the steps at night, and its jaws swinging open, dark and mysterious, to tempt me.

Really it was a squalid place, once you were inside. All its splendour was at the front for the street to admire. It always lured me in. And when you were inside you found half the seats broken, the curtains grey with dirt. The 'Exit' sign at the bottom, to the left of the screen, had a smashed glass and you could see the naked bulb. Above it squatted the clock, bathed in a red light, that would spin its hands round at a dizzy rate, whirling my happiness away.

I used to wait at the back entrance, at the mouth of a long covered ramp like a down-sloping tunnel, waiting to be taken in. This shabby picture house was my paradise. Nothing could keep me away. I would hang around for a long while, holding out my fourpence, watching the success of my friends with envious pangs. A small group of us gathered in the early evening, but through my timidity I was usually the last one in. Tears of resentment gathered in my eyes as I heard everyone gasping and screaming in perfect time. Often I would be on the point of giving up when some elderly person stopped out of kindness, without even being asked. I followed them as if they were gods.

To get my fourpence two or three times a week it was necessary to slink into the kitchen and beg it from my mother, standing back out of earshot of my father. I whispered to her guiltily, knowing she could never refuse me. I knew also that she could hardly afford it, and this knowledge filled me with shame— though not strongly enough to prevent me from asking again a few days later. I ran off along the street to join the others, smarting with remorse and vowing that my first act when I became an adult would be to make plenty of money and get my mother out of that kitchen. She seemed eternally chained in there, drudging away at some task for one of us.

Facing the cinema on the opposite corner stood my first Church of England school, where I had been happy. On my way home one night I dodged across to one of the windows. It had been damaged and boarded up. Nobody was about, so I peered in through the gaps. I found myself gazing into the semi-darkness of the wash-house, and could just make out two large shapes, like pale smudges looming out faintly. These were the two basins, grey with filth, where we used to mix the ink, flooding the black liquid over our hands, and also rinse out the milk bottles. I felt a fierce desire to see the scarred desks again, to sit in the old classroom and look up through the big high window at the poster advertising biscuits, glued to the red brick of the Acropolis. I would even have enjoyed seeing the headmaster once more, with his bald head and withered left hand. I remembered Miss Rutherford's bony, purple-veined hands, the fingers white with chalk, and her wrinkled neck, like a plucked fowl's, poking out of a shiny black dress.

I went on down the street. Then a swift flood of memory brought back the other names, each name unlocking its own tiny compartment of memory. George Williams rose up first, a figure of fear. As I pieced him together I still feared him, with his shaven, bullet head. He swaggered about the playground, the born bully, whirling his arms like windmills as he walked towards you. Only Tony Miller opposed him, an erect black-headed boy who strode unhurriedly, marching and arrogant, his back held stiff, making me tingle with pride and worship. The dunce of the class, Doreen, wore ugly steel spectacles, behind which her soft round eyes glazed and blinked with meaningless tears in her pock-marked face. Joyce Price was the favourite, flat-faced, bubbles of cleverness streaming from her mouth. She was bland and fish-like, swaying her head as she talked. Her legs were like tallow candles. She inched away from Jackie Dewar, who sat at the same desk and wore smelly corduroy breeches. "Stop picking your nose!" she hissed at him.

That night, as I was slinking into sleep, I thought, 'Why did I have to leave that school, where I was happy?'

ii

Each day, when I came home from school, I set the table for the evening meal. My father left the factory at a quarter past five, so there was plenty of time. It was one of a number of small jobs I did. I would usually be doing it, or just finished, when my uncle Dennis arrived. He worked on a night shift at another factory, and called in at our house on his way there. I came to take his curious upside-down life for granted. He walked in, sleepy and bleary-eyed, wearing a dark-blue beret, his hands gloved invisibly with the sweet-smelling ointment he wore to ward off the suds oil that was used on his machine. He was a machinist.

He liked to sit in our house for a while, and wake up. It was something he had been doing for years. He never talked much. A shy, dreamy man, still young, he would rake through his hair with long lean fingers, yawning. The yawn ended as a smile at my mother. She was ready to nag him, and he invited her.

On Sundays he gave me lessons on the violin, and during the week I stood practising by myself, in the musty, museum-like smell of our front room. I made my chin sore with practice, scraping with great care and energy to produce my first complete tune, 'Twinkle, twinkle, little star', learning by trial and error to avoid the worst accidents. The scales were rushed through, then I went over and over this tune, feeling quite proud, until my mother yelled through the wall: "You're driving me mad with that star!"

Dennis treated me like a man.

"How's it going?" he asked.

I would answer gruffly, in the same manner: "Not bad, thanks."

He sat drinking hot tea, lifting the steaming liquid in spoonfuls at first, fastidiously, pouting his lips to blow. His long legs would be crossed, tucked under his chair, like a bird roosting.

"That's a bachelor's trick," my mother said, watching him.

"What is?"

"What you're doing."

"Go on." He laughed his shy, boy's laugh. "Rubbish."

"It's true."

His eyes gleamed, and I knew he was about to say something witty.

"How about if I drink it from a saucer?" he asked, with a bantering intonation. "That any better? Will that keep me young for ever, like Peter Pan?"

"Laugh, then," my mother said. "You'll find out."

While he sat there I ran his errands, fetching cigarettes and a newspaper, and posting his letters. On Friday evening, as I stood holding out his change, he pretended to be absorbed in the newspaper.

"How much left?" he asked, his head lowered.

"Tenpence."

"Keep it."

The arrival of my father was a signal for him to set out. Also, around this time, I was expected to find my grandfather, in the park or the public reading-room, and tell him to come in for his meal.

I went to the reading-room first. If he was not there, I looked at the periodicals for a while. This quickly bored me, and I soon began to glance round at the people. Some were standing, some leaning, one or two seated at long tables, and one at least would be asleep, arms and head huddled on the table. They were mostly old men, I noticed. In the summer there were only a few, but in the winter they came in out of the cold, sheltering from the wind, and the room was always crowded. If there had been a stove, I imagine they would have abandoned the pretence of reading and gathered round it, huddling together in their dirty macs and overcoats. They turned the dog-eared sheets of newsprint slowly, falteringly, without much interest.

It was a big, bare room, dark even in summer, and the electric lights burned continuously, high up, lost in the gloom. I often felt, walking in suddenly from the street, that I had interrupted a secret meeting, and as I stepped into the place they all stopped what they were doing and pretended to read. Some of them stared at me openly, as if in anger, and I should have felt ashamed of being only a few years old, in comparison with them, if it had not been for my grandfather. He made it necessary for me to go there.

In the winter he was usually there, sitting at a table, dozing, though still upright, his cherry-coloured stick laid in front of him, under one hand.

At five o'clock, when I went in, I always recognised the same faces. For instance, there was a man of fifty or so who always sat turning the pages of a magazine as he gazed leisurely around, his mouth curved in a crafty smile, his eyes extraordinarily sad and gentle. Another man often leaned half out of his chair, twisted away from the table, his cap slipping down over one eye. He seemed to be snoring when I arrived, but if he was really asleep, how did he manage to stay rigid in that falling position? Occasionally I caught a glimpse of his seamed face, brown and marked all over, like worm-eaten wood, screwed up in a terrifying blind squint.

One old fellow in particular fascinated me. He dragged a stiff leg—perhaps an artificial one—and went from paper to paper as though he meant to devour every line of print in the place. He wiped his eyes, and thrust his shrunken face forward, almost rubbing against the sheet. I could hear his breath rasping in and out like a rusty bolt.

First of all he went the round of the newspapers fixed on the wooden stands against the walls. Then he started on the magazines. He missed nothing, working methodically from table to table, reading everything. His hands had great swollen veins, like worms, and ancient, splitting nails. Though he was very thin and starved-looking he had these huge hands, that seemed to be feeding on his body.

I was sitting there one afternoon, bored with things, and found myself watching an ugly incident. It was begun by a big man at one end of the stands who lost his temper, a sort of business man, with a thick bull neck, criss-crossed, hide-like skin, and a soft tweed hat, like a fisherman's, which flopped round his ears. I remember particularly his neck and hat. His back was towards me, and a scrawny fellow, wearing glasses and a cloth cap, stood by his side. He looked over Bull Neck's shoulder, a little to his left, patiently waiting his turn. His back and dangling hands had a meek look. I must have missed the first move, for when I looked up this man was staggering backwards, and Bull Neck had yelled out in the silent room: "Get off! Clear out!"

Everybody stopped reading. The thin man had gone white at the lips, but he went back, his eyes blinking rapidly behind his spectacles.

"Hey, what's the idea?" I heard him ask softly, and he stood there again. The big man went yellow with strange rage, slobbering with fury. I thought he was in a sort of fit.

"Get away! Wait your bloody turn!"

This time he had turned, planted his large hand on the other man's chest and pushed with his full weight, lunging forward.

"Go on, get out of it."

His ugly words hung in the silence. The quiet man's glasses had slipped across his face as he staggered back about six yards and nearly fell. It was all somehow more horrible because they were both middle-aged.

I wanted somebody to interfere, or the man to walk away. He was replacing his glasses and straightening his clothes. He went back, like a victim, and stood there again. He was deathly white, and I heard him say in a faint, shaky voice, "You keep your hands off me."

He glanced down at his feet and made a slight movement to the left, as if objectively resuming the same position.

Bull Neck was beaten now. He had not foreseen such dogged persistence, such disregard for brute force. All his cruelty was written in that ugly creased neck, red and thick. He waited a few minutes, vindictive, apprehensive, plainly wondering what to do next. Then he swung round and made a theatrical gesture, full of insult, hanging his bulk over the other man.

"It's all yours, my friend!" he bawled into the silence. "Next time, don't breathe down my neck—got that?"

He swaggered self-satisfied down the room, watchful for signs of approval or opposition, muttering to himself. The gaunt man stepped in front of the paper and began to read, and everything was as before, as though nothing had happened.

### iii

One wintry day, as I sat looking round, the men seemed older than ever. Some I had never seen before. Perhaps the exceptionally cold weather drove them in. Beside them my grandfather could hardly be called old at all. Surrounded by these worn-out, dried-up bodies that creaked and complained with every move, by withered heads nodding on thin, scraggy stalks of necks, by toothless dribbling mouths, tortoise skins, and eyes that were acute and bird-like, or watery and bewildered—I felt like a foreigner. I almost felt like a trespasser, and of another race—as if I had broken into one of their secret haunts, where they did not wish to be seen or disturbed. Surely my presence there was like laughter in their faces, the mocking laughter of past days?

I overheard conversations, and sometimes became involved in them, young as I was. One afternoon a man sitting opposite me kept putting a hand up to his face and rubbing it over his cheek with a sound like dry papers scraping together. He wasn't one of the really old ones. His jacket was fastened at the neck with a safety-pin, and the cuffs were so frayed that I could not help staring at them. His face looked hungry, thin and sharp, with a fat swollen nose leaking into his moustache. His other hand, blue with cold, kept turning the thumbed, tattered pages of his periodical. I could smell his sweat.

"Cold!" his companion said beside him, watching me and winking. His flat, comical face was covered with lines.

"Cold!" once again. Then: "Had your dinner?"

"Don't eat no dinner," said the one facing me. He rubbed his face and sighed, then turned over another page.

"I'm feelin' awful," he went on, not bothering to raise his head. "Feelin' awful. Ever feel awful?"

Was he talking to me, or his friend? I tried to see what he was reading, or rather, what he had in front of him. The inverted letters which headed the page were like a puzzle. At last I had it: *The Accountant's Journal.*

He was talking to himself.

"Goin' to get some fish and chips today . . . got to have somethin' . . . Don't need dinners when I'm feelin' all right . . . Feelin' awful . . ."

His head began nodding drowsily.

Where did he go when he left here, I wondered. Were there any other free places? He could only sit in the park, the icy wind slapping round his ankles. He could sit there as long as he liked, enjoying the bright sun, though it would be months before there was any warmth in it. It was the end of December.

"Happy New Year!" croaked his companion suddenly, and an imbecile cackle of laughter burst from him. "You, I mean—you!" he cried, leaning sideways and poking with his leathery finger, trying to get a response, and as he did so, staring across at me, swivelling his big yellow face.

But this man facing me refused to pay attention. He was holding his head between both his hands, sitting motionless. 'He's asleep,' I told myself, not wishing to think of him as ill.

Only once did I see that old man in there who stalked about Woodfield with long, slow strides, majestic as an Egyptian king—though I often saw him in the streets. He seemed oblivious of the stares and gapes and giggles. I cannot remember ever seeing disdain or anger on his face. He cast a spell by the very grace of his walk. People were bound to mock him. He wore dilapidated kid gloves, his coat was green on the shoulders, a wavy greyish mane of hair flowed down from his hat, touching his collar, and he had a huge, lush beard. His face was clean and apple-cheeked.

In the summer months, on my way home from the park, I sometimes passed him standing at the top corner of Market Street. A large brown-paper parcel was tucked under his arm. I heard people say that this contained his belongings. Going past one night I overheard a woman offering him some money.

"Here, get yourself a cup of tea," she said.

He didn't move. He stood like a statue.

"No, I don't want it," he said, very clearly.

And the woman hurried off in confusion. What kind of tramp was he, refusing money? Was he just standing there to admire the view, or what? Was that all he could find to do? I expect that was what she thought. Each time I saw him I was so impressed that I wanted to stop and speak. But what could I have said?

iv

I spent a good deal of my time at week-ends in the park, which was not far from our house. It spread over the top of a small hill which rose up suddenly out of the streets, like a green wave. If I stood on the highest mound of this park, against the railings, I could look down into our street, caught firmly in the twisted net of all the others.

I met my grandfather's friend here, Francis, a little man who had managed to strike up a conversation with my grandfather in the reading-room, despite the barrier of his deafness, and ever since had sat with him in the park, on one of the iron benches. Whenever he spotted my grandfather he came trotting across and sat next to him, and started chattering. Perhaps he was unaware of the deafness, or perhaps he didn't care about it. If the old man was elsewhere and Francis caught sight of me, he used to call me over.

He wore the same overcoat in all weathers, a dark one which was several sizes too large, and his thin neck looked comical, springing out of the loose gaping top of it. I doubt if he was over fifty, but he had no teeth, so that his cheeks and mouth were sunken, making him appear much older. He was even smaller than my grandfather, a frail leaf of a man, with bony ankles, and his ears stood out almost at right angles to his head. The first time

he called me over he began at once to tell me all his troubles, as if
it had been arranged that I should deputise for my grandfather. I
noticed his eyes, and because of them I had difficulty in attending
to what he was saying. I had never seen such bright eyes.

"I'm living with my brother and his wife, you see, but they're
getting fed up with me!" he said in a quavering voice. "They keep
telling me I shall have to find somewhere else. I don't know, I'm
sure. There don't seem to be any work about, to speak of. I've
looked everywhere. I've got a rupture, you see, that's the trouble.
I've got this rupture. Nobody'll have me when they know that.
It's a proper devil!" He began to wheeze and gasp with soundless
laughter. "I'm hanged if I know what to do. I got it lifting a heavy
casting off the floor, at the last place I was at ... I'm not saying
anything against my brother and his wife, it's not their fault—I
can't expect them to keep me for nothing, or next to nothing, can
I? I don't like to stay there when I know I'm being a burden—but
what else can I do? She's a nice woman and all that, a very nice
woman, but ... well, she doesn't give me enough to eat. I'm
walking along some mornings and I suddenly go all dizzy and
have to sit down. I shall have to do something soon, it's no good,
I shall have to raise the wind somehow. I don't know, I'm sure!"

He kept breaking off into a queer disembodied chuckle, blinking his bright eyes. Once or twice he ceased talking altogether,
hanging his head, as though he had become very absorbed in his
blue canvas shoes. Perhaps he had. He was making his toes move
inside them, lifting each toe in turn, bulging the canvas tops.

There was a sore place on one of his fingers, which he examined periodically. He peered at it more intently, while his free
hand groped in the pocket of his overcoat. He pulled out a big
khaki handkerchief, and a number of articles came out with it
and fell to the ground: a needle and a thread, the stub of a pencil,
and a tin of ointment.

"Ah, that's one thing I was looking for," he quavered, picking
up the tin. He did not seem to notice the other things. Fumbling
in one of his pockets again, he brought out a packet of sticking
plasters.

"What a life!" he mumbled. He chuckled to himself. "What a
bloody life!" His hand shook. His trembling fingers were strug-

gling to open the packet, and as I watched him I held my breath. 'It's going to fall!' I told myself. At that moment the tin of ointment slipped out of his lap and fell on the gravel once more. It rolled, so I jumped down and picked it up.

"Shall I do it?" I asked, with the tin in my hand. I took out one of the plasters from the packet on his lap, and Francis held out his finger. I put it on carefully. "How's that?" I asked.

"That's very kind of you, young man. Thank you, thank you very much."

A tiny crackle of laughter came out of his mouth, involuntarily, from the leaf of his body. He brimmed over with silent hilarity, looking at me, and only this barely audible crackling sound came out of him. It was all he could manage.

I had never seen eyes as bright as this man's. I marvelled at them. They had a confused, bewildered expression, and their brightness was uncanny, not natural.

"Would you like to see this newspaper?" Francis said. He rummaged in his pockets again, even unfastening his overcoat. "If I can find it—I know I've got it here somewhere!"

As I watched him I thought, "He must have everything in those pockets." I was beginning to like this queer man, and wondered how he managed to remain so cheerful when his position seemed so desperate. While he ransacked his pockets I studied his face, as though the secret of his cheerfulness lay buried there, like a treasure.

He drew out the paper from an inner pocket and unfolded it, flattening it on his lap with the palm of his hand before giving it to me. It was over a week old, but I pretended to read it. I found my eyes wandering off to the large patches of earth in front of us, where the grass was worn, and I wondered vaguely how many hundreds of feet must have trampled the grass, for that to have happened.

I had been day-dreaming, for Francis was on his feet. He swayed unsteadily.

"Cheerio, young man," he said, and then he crackled with laughter.

I smiled at him.

"Cheerio," he repeated.

But he did not attempt to move. He stood still, and I was forced to look at him. An extraordinary smile spread over his tiny face. He chuckled once more and blinked his eyes. I found myself laughing, for no reason at all. We seemed to understand each other. I laughed again.

Francis shuffled off over the grass, his overcoat, which he had forgotten to fasten, flapping round his legs, and I noticed his weakly jutting knees. He was unsteady on his feet. I watched him until he was out of sight. Where was he off to now?

A gust of cold wind came across the bare park and made me shiver. It was early March. I saw some friends in the distance, and ran across to them.

v

Two days later I saw him again; then he was missing for about three weeks. The next time I saw him I went across to his seat, sitting down by his side. His long absence had made me curious about him.

"Hallo," I said.

He looked me full in the face, not recognising me. His head rocked about on his neck, and though his eyes were brighter than ever, he could hardly speak. When he tried it was painful to watch him. A tiny froth clung to his lips. He screwed up his eyes and wrinkled his forehead, as though he were struggling to remember something, and now the gentle expression on his face had disappeared. His face was dirty and rough with beard.

"Are you all right?" I asked.

I bent over the man, half-afraid, and saw that his face was covered in faint, dull blotches. He was slobbering a little from the corners of his mouth, and kept closing his eyes, as if the eyelids were too heavy to support. His chin fell on to his chest like a bit of dry wood, his head nodding, sinking lower and lower. Then he jerked it up, almost angrily. His eyes were like bright beads, sunk back in his head.

"Are you all right?" I asked again. "Don't you remember me?"

The man lifted his head. His chin wobbled. "I feel sleepy," he mumbled in a whisper.

He clutched the edge of the seat with both hands and stood up. Then he staggered, his hands pawing the air. I grasped his elbow to steady him, before he shuffled away.

I watched him anxiously. What was the matter with him? Surely he was ill? It was unsafe for him to be walking about the streets in that condition. He could fall under a bus. Somehow I felt responsible for him, and for a moment I thought of running to fetch my grandfather. But Francis had disappeared—it was too late for that. I pictured the man's glistening eyes, too bright, and that confused, harassed look in them. One of the things he told me came to my mind, which struck me at the time as a strange expression. "I've been thrown on the scrap-heap." I had never heard it used before. I went on to visualise him wandering out over the main road, and then the accident, and suddenly I wanted to run after him and call "Hi! Wait a minute!" to delay him. Instead, I concentrated on a woman who had come into view, with an Alsatian dog following at her heels. The woman held a gaudy rubber ball, and as I watched she jerked back her arm and flung the ball far out over the grass. The dog leapt up, then plunged forward powerfully, ploughing through the air as if it were breasting a river; the ball bounded ahead like spray. Slowly the woman strolled towards me, swinging a leather lead.

When she had gone past I jumped up and wandered in the direction Francis had taken.

I came to a small crowd, clustered round a park bench near one of the entrances. What took my eye first was a bicycle, placed against a tree-trunk. It had a big square frame, gleaming black, with a double crossbar for extra strength, and stood propped there, big and important, like a gate on wheels. It was enormous. I realised after a few moments why it was that size. It belonged to a policeman who was bending over somebody half-hidden by two or three onlookers. I pushed my way in, and there was Francis, slumped in one corner of the seat like a bundle of old clothes. His eyes fluttered open, the lids trembled delicately, like butterflies. The policeman arched lower, and I looked quickly at his white bony face under the high, jug-shaped helmet. He was whispering questions as he loosened the man's collar with long spatulate fingers.

"Have you been taking anything, Francis?" he was saying. "That is your name, isn't it? It is Francis, isn't it? Eh? And what's your other name? Can you hear me, Francis? What have you been taking? Did you want to do away with yourself? Been having a bit of trouble? Are these the tablets, in this bottle, Francis?"

Somebody in the crowd said: "Where's that ambulance?"

The man on the seat tried to speak.

"I—I . . . can't . . . stand up," he whispered, and his head sank forward. The movement pressed a faint crackling breath out of his body.

"Tell me your other name," the policeman urged softly. "Tell me where you live. Can you remember? What is your name, Francis?"

"Yes," the man said, suddenly. He sighed.

"Tell me then, old man. Tell me, there's a good chap."

The policeman stooped, lowering his head, waving at the group to be silent as he listened.

"Tell me," he said.

The man made a tremendous effort. His lips moved. They seemed to be coated with a whitish paste.

"Francis," he said at last, faintly. And the policeman straightened his back.

"That's fine, old chap," he said, and gave the little crowd a brisk, sharp look, as if he expected laughter.

I forced my way out.

"What's the matter with the old boy?" somebody hissed in my face.

"I don't know."

"Can't he stand up?" asked another person. "Is he drunk?"

"I don't know!" I shouted, and ran away.

Later on, we read in the local *Telegraph* that a man named Francis Beresford had been taken to hospital after collapsing in the park. He had died the same day.

# Three

i

Not long after this I started work, and brought home my first pay-packet. It was a proud moment, even though I could only hand my mother just over ten shillings. On the way home that Thursday I bought a newspaper, and came in smacking it against my leg like an adult.

My father had arranged for me to become an apprentice at the car factory in the city where he was employed as an upholsterer. Only I was to be an engineer. It was a huge maze of a place, like a great shed roofed with glass, full of shafts and flapping belts. Private roads were cut through, and even a railway. When I could find my way about I used to go over to the upholsterers' shop every afternoon for a few minutes and talk to my father, waiting for him to empty his mouth of tacks. As his hammer struck accurately his left hand rose to the tack glinting between his lips.

It was much cleaner where he worked, and less noisy because of the absence of machinery. I envied him, but I knew he had done his best for me by putting me to the other trade. His trade was dying out, he explained. Before long they would invent machinery to do it. It was too uncertain, he said, and shook his head dolefully.

All the same, I soon realised that I should never become an engineer. Perhaps outwardly I might, but not at heart—my heart wasn't in it. But I had no idea what I really wanted to do, so I did my best to avoid the subject. It confused me. I did not want to decide anything. As a matter of fact, I only wanted to be left alone, like my grandfather—which I knew was not very practical. I was too dreamy, even then, and the world I found myself in, the factory-world, battered my day-dreams to pieces with its own violent unreality.

At first, though, it was far better than being at school. I was bringing home a pay-packet each Thursday, and no longer felt such a burden to the household. I regained my self-respect. And it was so different from the tyranny of school, which I had hated. I welcomed the easy, slack atmosphere. Nobody bothered you if you did your work. They left you to get on with it. I enjoyed the comradeship—if you could call it that—of the other lads of my own age. Working with your hands, labouring, you fell quite naturally into this comradeship. It was easy and slack and natural, with no depth to it. You picked it up casually every morning where you had left it the night before, like a discarded overall.

I was in my second year of apprenticeship when my grandfather did something that amazed us all. He found himself a job, at a small plating works only a few streets from our house. He had kept the idea a secret, not mentioning any desire to do such a thing, so it was quite unexpected.

Was there any reason for it? He shrugged his shoulders. The sight of me, thumping down a pay-packet every week, may have made him restless; and my wage, small as it was, did push him down a bit farther in importance, as far as earning capacity was concerned. With me at work he was on a level with my sister, which was preposterous. It may have been that. Or perhaps he became suddenly bored, and wanted something to do: suddenly restless, as old men are, sometimes, after a lifetime of activity. He refused to say what it was.

Now he came home at six in his stained clothes, reeking with the acid smell. No matter what he did, or how many times he washed, this pungent, sharp smell clung to him. It went with him everywhere. When he changed into his Sunday suit it was still there, rising in sharp whiffs from his hair.

In the mornings, now, before he set off for work, there was a new ritual. After giving him the insulin injection as usual, my mother had to bandage his arms with wide cotton gauze, almost to his armpits, for protection against burns and splashes. I always left first, and he would be sitting at the table, bent over a dish of cereal, pearling his thick moustache with milk and stretching out his hairy left arm for my mother to begin.

He had to work overtime one Saturday, and forgot to take his sandwiches. So in the afternoon I took them round to the plating shop. It was no distance. I went through the double gates into the little yard. On the damp cobbles were bunches of freshly plated nuts and bolts, wired together, and I had to pick my way through to reach the door of the shop. Steam came hissing out of a rusty pipe, high up on the building, and drifted out over the yard. They did different kinds of plating here, but the bunches of wired parts lying about all had the same matt coating of white cadmium.

A jovial fellow came out, his face broad, red as raw meat, to ask me what I wanted. As I told him I brandished my package in unconscious emphasis. I stood at the low door, and this man poked his head over my shoulder, behind me, and bellowed:

"Bert Chapman!"

Inside it was so badly lit and so full of steam that I could not recognise the old man among the other stooping figures. Then I saw him, bulky and stiff in a big yellow apron, rubber gloves and boots, bent over one of the vats, half obscured by a cloud of steam. He was dipping and lowering a wire basket with long handles, his face ruddy with heat.

"Deaf as a post," laughed the man behind me. He was the charge-hand. He pushed by and went lunging in between the vats, splashing through pools of orange water on the concrete floor. I saw him go up to my grandfather and press his shoulder, pointing towards me. The old man raised an arm then and waved. He attended to his basket and came clumping out, walking with slow, weighty strides, like a deep-sea diver. His rubber boots glistened all over with moisture.

"Brought me sandwiches?" he shouted, as we stood together in the daylight. The smell coming from him was very powerful. It stood solid in the air between us. I watched him dragging off one of the weird swollen gloves, the fingers like sausages.

I nodded vigorously.

"Good lad, good lad!" he said. The strong light was making him squint. I left him stuffing the package in his trouser-pocket.

When he struggled out of bed now in the mornings he cursed under his breath, sometimes grunting with pain. He was nearly seventy. But at week-ends he still kept up his hunt for bargains, and went on the double expedition to the shops and the market, never missing a Saturday.

ii

As the years passed, and I grew more and more dissatisfied with my job and the general trend of my life, I turned to books. I bolted them down with real hunger, reading indiscriminately. Also I became more critical of my workmates, and began to pass judgement on them: a sure sign that I was growing up. In a secret part of myself, a tiny, hidden, unacknowledged place, there was the desire to be a poet, or an artist of some kind, which I hugged and nourished, though sometimes the very thought of such a thing filled me with distaste and vague dread. I disliked the word 'poet' intensely; it sounded so foppish, and so far removed from life as I knew it.

Much later I got hold of Whitman from the library, and this old-fashioned book, its photographs protected with sheets of yellowing tissue paper, taught me that poetry could be quite a different thing. Later still I discovered Rimbaud. It was like a bomb bursting, impossible to understand, but tremendously reckless and exciting. In my first efforts I imitated them both, simultaneously. I was very shy and guilty and excited. They were ferocious, bloodthirsty things, those first poems of mine. They terrified me. My secret face stared out of them with such an obvious yearning, it seemed to me, that I hid them away in the chest of drawers, under a pile of papers. I didn't want my mother to read into my soul and see all the adolescent agony and lack of love. I shrank from the thought of it. Yet, on reflection, they were not personal poems, so that wouldn't have been possible. I hadn't written them in terms of myself, but of the world. It all distressed and disgusted me, when I saw how I had mixed my emotions so obviously into the state of the world. I didn't want that confusion.

Long before I realised the meaning of the word, I was a solitary. I used to glance at my reflection in plate-glass windows and groan at what I saw there. It was all written with humiliating clarity, the whole story, in that wincing, compressed mouth, on that startled, moon-like face. I hated my face for giving the game away, betraying me. But of course, being young, I also derived a good deal of mournful pleasure from it. I liked to think I was plunged in suffering.

Gradually I came to understand that art was comprised of misfits like myself. When I realised this fully, I wanted to wash my hands of it. It all seemed bound up with misunderstanding, failures, consumptives and crucified messiahs. I became so obsessed by the idea that poets and artists nearly always died of bleeding lungs that I began coughing into my handkerchief periodically, watching for signs. What a fate that would be, I thought grimly—to start spitting blood before I had even written a single good poem. Then suddenly the whole idea of poetry being connected in some sinister way with sickness and death disgusted me. I stopped spurring myself on, filled with apprehension, as if I had been swallowing poison unwittingly. Words were a snare, a quagmire, a deadly trap. My grandfather became an object of admiration now, an antique, sturdy figure, untouched by cleverness. I looked at him with new respect. How lucky he was to be such a simple man!

In books I sought out and fastened on to this uncouth, rugged quality. Carlyle was a great discovery; I read his *Heroes and Hero-Worship* from cover to cover, thrilled and ennobled. But Rimbaud kindled me in a different way. His very name sounded mysterious, and he was a boy when he wrote his poetry. That was the only real fact I knew about him. I tried to track down his life, but for a long time I could find nothing, and began to wonder if there was a conspiracy, a deliberate policy of some kind, to avoid mentioning his name. No doubt I even wished for such a thing. It made him dangerous and iconoclastic; not merely on paper, but in the real world. Such youthful casuistry sprang out of the hero-worship I brought to bear on him. I looked everywhere for oblique references to his name, and still found nothing. I thought once of approaching the young assistant at the reference library, yet I was afraid of mispronouncing the poet's name. Eventually, in a weighty encyclopædia there, I unearthed half a dozen lines, in which he was contemptuously dismissed. They had a rich, sunset magic, though they were really quite factual and dry in themselves. Reading them, a vision rose up of a one-legged beggar hobbling through the villages of France, a wild, scarecrow figure of a man, his shirt stuffed with poems, living in holes in the hillsides and scrabbling down in the night on all fours like a werewolf, friendless and hated.

My hunger grew, as I whetted my appetite on those early books. Meanwhile, my father was put in charge of a section at the factory, and soon after this we moved to another house, in a better district, where I had a little box-room to myself.

But I hardly noticed these things. For some, youth is like a whirlpool, or a labyrinth of pain and confusion. You are caught up and up and flung about, rushing along madly. Everything happens at once, within yourself. You keep turning inward, inward, and lose all humour. You even grow thin and ecstatic and your face changes. It is a stormy, difficult time, and before you are lifted out and dropped on the shore of a calmer place, getting up in wonder and relief, finding that you are a man, you can have known some madness.

Whirling through those years, I emerged once or twice, half-realised what was happening, then rushed on subjectively again. I knew one thing clearly. I knew I had left the magic world of my childhood for good, with its erect, splendid mornings. I knew I should never sit under that strange tree on the common again, where the branches and leaves came down to the ground all around me, a green light filtering through, so that I could sit on the damp turf against the trunk and imagine I was under the sea. For I had lost the clue to that world. More and more I should have to struggle against dreariness. Though adolescence could be just as intense and vivid as childhood, it was rarely simple. Nearly always it was discoloured, cloudy and turgid, full of embarrassment.

As I brooded on it in those days, cycling to work and returning home, I came to regard my acute shyness as almost a physical affliction which would throw me into spasms and fits like an epileptic, in a sudden attack. I saw myself as a victim in a self-conscious, paralytic world. I was only at ease with those whom I knew to be unobservant, the semi-illiterate working-class people of our district, and my mates at the factory. My dread of meeting strangers, my ruses and excuses to avoid parties and outings, conflicted sharply with my longing for contact, for real friendship.

Anyone in the least sensitive repelled me. I can only explain the extreme solitude of those years by this dread of facing strangers, and my refusal to 'mix', which my mother was always reproaching me for. Yet she was as bad at it herself, and, knowing the harshness of life, it dismayed her to see a recurrence of this trait in me. To her it seemed a serious handicap, almost a disaster, letting me in for an endless succession of knocks and bruises. She saw it as the root of my adolescent difficulties, yet she was power-less to help me. For my own part, I knew perfectly well how near I was to the stuttering neurotic of modern times.

Apart from poetry, I read a great deal of fiction now. I read the serial love stories in *John Bull* and *The Passing Show*, and began to ransack the library for anything that would describe to me the details of an encounter with a girl, a first approach. It seemed an unsurmountable problem, and though I had no desire to go with girls yet, I felt compelled to do something to train myself for this ordeal.

Of course the stories I read did nothing whatever to help me. They only shed a more powerful light on my predicament, which was the last thing I wanted. For I wanted desperately to coarsen myself, sink my consciousness into oblivion, throw my mind away, shut it off. I felt I was a skin short. Almost from the begin-ning I regarded my trouble as an 'affliction', and took it for granted that it was a typically modern one. Later, when I was steeped in Nietzsche, I cursed the fact of my nationality, blaming that, as if I had to have a scapegoat. And it seemed to me that no people anywhere in the world were as shrinking and self-conscious as the English, or so ashamed and in fear of their bodies. So I heaped abuse on them. They represented everything I did not wish to be. My heart bubbled like Nietzsche's with contempt and intoler-ance. I exalted the dark races because I could not imagine a more devastating contrast, lumping them all together naïvely.

With typical seriousness, too, I gave my parents some search-ing glances, examining myself in relation to them. I took pride in my ruthless objectivity. But what I saw only bewildered me, especially when I subjected *their* fathers and mothers to the same analysis. Where did I cease to be myself, where did they cease to be themselves? Their qualities flowed to and fro, and spun a baffling web. I recognised bits of myself in them all, but these faint resemblances couldn't give me the clue I sought. I wanted to know, plainly and simply, where I went off the rails and became such a wretched misfit.

My mother and father were complex personalities; I found that I hardly knew them. I had always thought of them as simple folk. But now we were strangers. My mother's gentle tolerance, excessive timidity and vague religiosity only formed one facet of her character. A shrewd, wry humour lurked under the shy exterior, and a powerful, unswerving will lay deeper still, a stubborn immovable core which would never admit failure. And my father, with his mildly scornful atheism, his naïve earnestness and innocence, he was a strange bafflement of modernity, socialism, progress, and a childlike eager unworldliness that kept brimming up in bright fountains, in vigorous shining enthusiasms, only to fall back, baffled; so that he was thrown into dark apathetic moods, into sullen broodings and silences. Then my mother would call him 'pig-headed' in her exasperation. She seemed to hate him, to want to attack him. But he only looked at her, his mouth smiling faintly, giving a bitter little smile, as if from a great distance. Nothing would make him speak.

### iii

I forced myself into a few adventures with girls, feeling humiliated by my lack of knowledge, and wanting some worldly experiences to boast about. All my workmates were experienced. In other ways I took care to behave like everybody else, but in this I was sadly lacking.

These adventures were short and disastrous. Each one was more distasteful than the last. It was better to be thought odd, I decided, and put up with the gibes of the other fellows. As I made the decision I felt wonderfully relieved.

Then I began to feel uneasy. Was I really a coward? Was I afraid of girls? I made one more attempt. A girl from the wages office often passed through the machine shops, walking briskly down the straight gangways between the white lines, past the piles of castings. I used to watch her from a distance. She was tall and boyish, with dark, bubbly hair. There was something attractive about her little narrow figure and brisk walk.

I asked Doreen, one of the good-natured factory women who worked nearby, if she would try to find out her name.

"That's Lena," she said immediately. "I know her."

Doreen was renowned for her skill in pairing off lads and girls. "Go and have a word with her," was always the advice, "she'll fix you up."

I gave her a note to pass to Lena. Within twenty minutes Doreen called me across to her bench, her eyes gleaming with triumph.

"She don't know you from Adam, she says, but she'll meet you on the corner at dinner-time, on the way back from work."

At the corner, a hundred yards from the factory, I paced up and down, watching for buses. It was a busy cross-roads, and I did not know which arm of traffic to watch, having no idea where she lived. I wished I had never made such a ridiculous arrangement.

Then it was too late to do anything, for she had jumped down from a bus as it drew level with the pillar-box. I struggled to pull myself together as the girl stood looking round gravely. I was appalled, now that the moment had come, and went forward jerkily, like a condemned man. It must have seemed odd to an onlooker.

"I'm Nick Chapman," I announced painfully. It sounded like a croak of despair. "I hope you don't mind the note—it was a cheek. I know."

"Oh, that's quite all right," she said brightly. "I'm late, aren't I. Hadn't we better be going in?"

As we passed the car park and the pub, drawing nearer to the factory gates, I asked if she would meet me one evening. We were mingling with a thick stream of workers, and I was afraid that somebody would recognise me.

"When?" she said archly.

"Is Tuesday any good?" My throat was dry.

"No, I'm afraid I can't manage that," Lena said blandly.

"Wednesday?"

The word dropped to the ground, naked as a stone. I hated it.

"I'm not sure. Ask me to-morrow, will you?"

She laughed hurriedly and ran in through the separate office entrance.

The next day I met her in the same way, and she gave me her address. Her voice grated on my nerves a little. There was a genteel, commonplace quality in it. Her teeth were slightly discoloured with nicotine. She was better at a distance, but I would not let myself dislike her.

On Wednesday evening I presented myself at her house, standing with a tense face in the summer jungle of front garden. I ought to have worn a tie, I thought as I waited, very conscious of my open white shirt and long exposed throat. Then the door was opened by Lena's thick-haired brother.

He stood back politely, looking wide-eyed at this new catch of his sister's. Both of them were about twenty-two or three, and their mother had been killed in a road accident during the war. Now Lena and her brother lived in the upper half of the house, letting the ground floor to relatives. When I saw them together they made me think of two brothers. They drifted in and out without regard for each other, though in all their speech there was something casual and brotherly, the insinuating, intimate sound that blood relations often have in their voices, and which a stranger finds so irritating.

I followed the young man upstairs. He ran up expertly, too fast for me. On the landing he waited, laughing and amiable, showing his small teeth.

I sat in the living-room while Lena fussed around me. There was a smell of gas which had seeped in from somewhere. Her brother wandered off discreetly into another room, getting ready to go out.

"Say, Dave," she called, as she stood in front of the mirror, "what time will you be back?"

"No idea," he drawled. "Why?"

"Got your key?"

"Somewhere," he said indifferently.

Lena watched me through her mirror. Then she began to search for a missing packet of cigarettes, twitching at her red organdie dress.

"Aren't I awful, keeping you waiting like this," she said, with naïve affectation. "What will you think of me?"

"Doesn't matter," I said out of my taut throat.

Her brother shuffled his feet, coughed, then poked his head round the door, a broad-minded grin on his face.

"I'm off then, Sis," he said. He gave me a sly look.

"Ta-ta!" she sang, not looking up.

On the way to the cinema we did not find much to talk about. I kept dragging in the factory as a subject, out of desperation. It had become a farce, just something to be got through as quickly as possible, now that I knew how commonplace she was. Each time she spoke I felt priggish, ashamed of my intelligence.

At the gate of her house, in the darkness, I realised that she expected me to do the conventional thing and kiss her goodbye. I could not bring myself to do it. Under the lamps, as we approached the house, I saw her small lifted face, smooth and complacent. I felt no desire for her. I kept thinking of a remark she had made earlier in the evening.

"Sometimes, when I think that I've got to die," she said, "I wish I'd never been born."

She spoke in such a simple, puzzled voice, like a child, that I felt pity for her.

"Don't you believe in heaven?" I asked, joking.

"I dunno," she said seriously.

Then in an instant her mood had changed, and she asked me if I ever went to dances. I told her I had never learnt.

"Do you object to girls going in pubs?" she asked abruptly and comically.

"No, I don't think so," I laughed.

There was an awkward silence. She lit another cigarette.

"I'm a shocking chain-smoker," she confessed. "I get through pounds and pounds." It sounded like a boast.

Suddenly she looked directly into my face, and I suppose I must have flinched.

"Are you self-conscious?" she asked curiously. The word sounded stupid in her mouth, as if she had read it somewhere and only half-understood its meaning, but it made me wince and stiffen, and go swinging back home later in fierce anger, with tight lips.

My mother watched me in silence as I dropped into a chair. She read the whole story in my face; it was becoming a familiar one. I sat stiffly, resisting her look, and she sighed and went on with her work.

"What a problem you are," she said once, in bitter reproach.

"Why should I be?" I said furiously. "You make a problem when there isn't one. Why do I have to be the same as other sons? Is that what you want?"

"No," she said, and seemed to wilt in her chair.

I felt cornered by her love, and longed to make her happy, but I could not bear the reproach in her voice.

"Then why am I a problem?" I demanded. Hatred flooded into my heart, black and obscure, as I sat facing her.

"You are, that's all," she said, and began to cry. "You are, you are," she said through her hands, in a strange, suffocating voice.

## iv

While I was still an apprentice I became friendly with a young fellow, an inspector, who affected an air of elegance. His name was Eric Lanyon. He had been an apprentice himself, and I got to know him when I worked on his section, before being transferred to another part of the factory.

He stood at a cluttered bench all day tinkering with delicate components, using long slender tools. It was a skilled, aristocratic sort of job, very specialised and important-looking, though I knew from experience that it was not too difficult. It hardly soiled his hands. He wore a white smock, and looked more like a dentist than an engineer.

Somehow I told him of my fondness for plays, a thing I rarely told anyone, and that was really how he came to befriend me. He had read a few 'highbrow' plays, Bernard Shaw, Chekov, Ibsen, and so on, and let me know that he took the *Spectator* every week. All this set him apart, as did his spotless overall and gleaming tools. He was artistic, and talked to me because he thought I was superior. I did not mind; I rather enjoyed his confidences at first. My vanity was being flattered.

At this time I operated a lathe, a good distance from his bench, but he always came across when he wanted to talk about intellectual things. He was fond of the word 'agnostic', using it whenever he could, and he considered himself a radical in a vague, lofty sort of way.

I never understood why he had such a high regard for my opinions. I could almost feel him envying me. His role in the conversation usually took the form of casual questioning, as he fished adroitly for my judgement of some book he had just read. Often I had no knowledge of it, but I was hardly ever stuck for a suitable comment. If it was Shaw I would say "Dead brains—dried up with his own intellect", or some such thing, hoping it covered that particular book. Lanyon had no ideas of his own, and his eyes opened wide with astonishment and delight at my vindictive remarks, as I demolished some human writing machine I despised. Then a knowing, appreciative smile rose on his face.

It was all done so pleasantly and humbly, his questioning, so patient and apologetic, and so unlike anything that had happened to me before, that it was impossible not to be pleased. It seemed incredible. To think of someone asking for my opinion! It almost went to my head. I kept raking about for brilliant, penetrating things to say, and my condemnations became more ruthless and crushing.

Later I realised how trite it all was, and got tired of Lanyon. I was not speaking freely to him, but talking like a puppet, jerked by his strings of questions. As a person I didn't like anything about him. For instance, I disliked his shirts. The collars were always faultless. That seemed characteristic of him. Also, I disliked his crisp, curly brown hair, so short and clean and efficient-looking. Even his refined, ever-pleasant face, smooth and fresh, with never a sign of a bristle, annoyed me, with its clear babyish forehead. And he had a pensive, poetic way of staring into space which irritated me more than anything else. As he spoke he would direct his gaze at the blue fog which always hung over a group of machines about twenty yards ahead of us, where they used gallons of sickly-smelling cutting oil. He gazed out dreamily, sucking his empty pipe, as if he found the view enchanting. It was his lack of realism that I found so hard to bear.

He was infinitely forgiving and magnanimous, and so polite, so sensitive, that I wanted to kick him. Sometimes I wondered if I looked at a reflection of myself when I looked at him. It made me go cold to think of it.

I went over to him once, as a concession, and as I stood there listening to his slow winding questions, he suddenly broke off. "Will you excuse me a moment, Nicholas," he asked gently, and turned to attend to a workmate, becoming superior and condescending. He used my full Christian name, which I hated, at every interruption, and excused himself each time. It sounded so ridiculous that I didn't go to him again. I made him come across to me.

If someone nearby let out a stream of foul language he would turn his head very slightly, contract his nostrils a little, and treat me to his most confiding look, a look which said: "What scum surrounds us here—but you understand!"

I guessed what it was all leading to. In a weak moment I had told him that I tried to write poems, and after this his visits became more frequent. One day I saw him picking his way delicately across the machine shop towards me, a strange excited gleam in his eye. For weeks he had been hinting at some verse of his own that he would like me to read. I kept hoping he would forget it. I didn't want to see his heart laid bare. But when I saw the enchanted smile on his face as he came up to me I knew the moment had come.

He was extremely embarrassed by the squalid, uncongenial surroundings, with the foul talk washing around us, and the din, but I looked coldly at him, hardening myself in readiness. What a fool he was, I thought. Why didn't he hug his secrets?

"They're nothing, nothing really," he said. "Mere doggerel. I just thought you—er—might—" and he laughed shyly, dropping the papers on the top of my toolbox, before paying a great deal of attention to his pipe. My hands were black with cast-iron dust, so I made that my excuse for not reading them immediately, and he left them with me.

When he was out of sight I wiped my hands and read quickly.

They were stilted, corpse-like things, encrusted with wordy metaphors, and a sort of combination of Heine and Oscar Wilde, with some psychological words sprinkled in to make them contemporary. I turned back almost in relief to the lathe and the cast-iron.

v

After this I felt I had had enough of words. There was a small table under the window in my box-room, and I sat up there, night after night, trying to paint water-colours. I chose street scenes for my subject matter, and turned to Rouault for my inspiration. I did not imitate his work deliberately, and I had only seen one painting of his reproduced in colour; but in a way, perhaps it was a furtive sort of imitation, relying on my faulty memorising of his work. Without troubling about technique I strove to saturate my water-colours with that religious fervour I loved, in which the colours burned and smouldered, glowing like fierce sunsets, and moved me to awe. For the first time I felt that painting was a ritual act, the colours belonging to all the carnival of life and death, as they did in Rouault. But I could capture neither his magnificent lambency nor any of his sombre power.

Why did I want to paint like him? Was it because he redeemed and transformed the ugliness in his compositions? When I thought of him, or of Van Gogh in the Borinage, I always saw a figure kneeling in a street with his head bared, praying in an inexplicable ecstasy.

One day, feeling that I should never get anywhere, I sought out a group of painters I had heard of, who called themselves the Birmingham Twelve. They were amateurs, and their leader was Cecil Luce, who often exhibited at local shows. When I obtained his address I plucked up courage and cycled across the city with a roll of water-colours to show him. In some obscure way I thought he might be able to help me.

I propped my bicycle against the pavement edge, outside his shabby semi-detached prefab, with its neglected garden and chocolate paint, and pushed open the gate. A man was in the front room, and when I glanced in timidly through the curtainless window, on my way up the path, he appeared to be painting on the door of the room with a small brush. He took no notice of me.

My knock on the door echoed inside the house, and I stood there self-consciously, wondering what I would say. I began to hope that no one would hear, so that I could have an excuse for postponing the visit, and then the door opened.

It was the man I had seen in the room. He was in his shirt-sleeves, and smelled of beer. The pointed sable brush was still in his right hand, loaded with vermilion paint.

"Mr. Luce?" I faltered.

He stared down at my hand holding the roll of paintings. Then his eyes revolved slowly and reached my face. I was amused, and forgot my nervousness.

"Come in, will you," he muttered, his pulpy lips leering at me. I followed him like a lamb after a shepherd, into the room he had just left.

The room was quite ordinary and common, but everything was in confusion, with sheets of paper strewn everywhere. As I followed him in I tried to explain why I had come, but he made no response. Somehow it did not seem important now.

"Don't call me 'Mr.'," he said suddenly. "Everybody says Cecil around here."

It sounded curious. I almost looked around to see where everybody was.

"I see," I said primly, and felt foolish, but I could not bring myself to say his name.

"Sit down here," he said in his blurred voice, and revealed a chair by pushing a heap of papers off it. "Shan't be a minute, just want to finish this."

He went back to a sheet of paper which was pinned to the door, and began to make fastidious little pecks at it with his brush. His free hand was plunged deep in his trousers pocket. My eyes wandered about, and I saw how the door was splashed and daubed in rectangles of various sizes, where other sheets had been pinned up and then removed.

I sat watching him, fascinated. He had a blind, heavy back, that looked as if all feeling had gone dead in it. His head flowed straight out of his neck, like a reptile's, slanting forward a little from the shoulders, so that he seemed to be sniffing the air. From behind he gave an impression of lowness; there was a thick, reptilian quality about him. I imagined life oozing down through his loose body, a slow clogging sub-life that moved with reluctance, like thick mud in a sack.

This was a new world to me. Cecil Luce was the first artist I had met. Instead of being thrilled I felt full of vulgar curiosity. Cecil's paintings were hung about on the walls, dry abstract compositions that meant nothing to me. I sat looking round, trying to connect them with this coarse slouching man, with his back of dead flesh under the dingy striped shirt.

He put down his brush. Then he rescued another chair from beneath some debris and sat down facing me, letting his hands dangle between his knees. He was slightly drunk. I saw that he was a youngish, long-legged man, with sagging eyelids and ginger moustaches. He took a pair of glasses from a case and put them on before starting to speak. Now he looked oddly studious.

He began telling me the history of the rebels in Birmingham. They had broken away from the Midland Association because of sharp differences of opinion, quarrelling over the merits of contemporary art. He felt there should be absolute freedom of expression for anyone who wanted it. He went on and on, making this obscure quarrel sound like an event of national importance that shook the whole art world. But I wasn't bored. I began to enjoy myself, and almost felt like a fellow artist, as I sat listening and nodding, instead of a potential engineer. There was no need for me to talk, because Cecil was so full of himself. The words flowed on so easily that I kept losing the thread, and gave up trying to decide whether it was lies or truth, or an artful blend of both. I sat motionless, not daring to move, like a bird before a snake, never taking my eyes from his flabby fascinating mouth. It was telling me now that Cecil had been befriended by famous people many years ago, and that a businessman was beginning to make a collection of Cecil's paintings.

He went on talking solidly. He did not live by his painting. At the moment he was a storekeeper at one of the builders' merchants.

"Which one?" I asked, to show that I was attending to him.

"Pearsons," he said irritably. "Don't matter, does it?"

He showed me a selection of his earlier work, unrolling it on the floor as he whistled a dance tune. Some of them were the work of his young nephew Edwin, he explained, who was also a gifted artist, though he was at present in a Birmingham hospital. "He's mad, crazy—wonderful, mind you, but no discipline," he said laconically, blinking and leering at me. "Look at these, and these. Mad."

These 'mad' ones were not abstractions. They were dream pictures. Tall, dripping figures stood out, top-heavy and melodramatic, and strange unrecognisable animals hung in the air. The colours were nearly all repellent.

Cecil held out his hand suddenly, without ceremony, squatting on his haunches near my feet. I untied the string around my own efforts, and handed them to him. I began to feel uncomfortable. I was sure he would find them ridiculously crude. He laid them flat on the brown carpet and crouched over, flicking through at a tremendous rate until he found one which appealed to him. He held this away from his face, pondering, before going on.

"Good," he said under his breath, and nodded several times.

Then he snatched one up and lumbered to his feet, waving it triumphantly like a flag. "This is how you want to paint, lad. Like this—see? You've got it here. Rouault's your man, I'd say. These lines though—my God, they're flying about all over the place! No sense of balance, no composition, nothing. That's secondary, I can teach you that. I've been perfecting my own stuff for years. Masses and groups, light and dark, like algebra—I'll show you. But the feeling's there, the feeling, that's the thing. Powerful— that Rouault feeling. Gets me straight in the stomach every time, always affects me. Power. Listen, lad, let me tell you something now: if I saw this in an exhibition, this one, it'd stop me dead!"

I have never met anybody so different and irresponsible before. I soon began to warm to him. It was only when I looked again at his own paintings that my enthusiasm waned. They were meaningless, I thought, done in a spirit of sadness and vacuity. They were just manifestations of emptiness, like modern buildings, with hard cutting edges and flat vacant surfaces. I fought them away almost in fear, not wanting to be contaminated by that dead spirit. For I had only one sure way of judging: I asked that my feelings be stirred, my compassion. If a painting failed to do this I rejected it. Yet the expensive folio of Ben Nicholsons which Cecil opened for me now so lovingly I thought magnificent. The colours were delicate and beautiful. But after a day or so I found myself untouched by them; they could have been non-existent.

As he showed me his treasures I looked at him. I noticed his thick, blunt fingers, his ugly hands, and the coarse greyish skin of his city-bred face, with its drained, shut-away look, and marvelled at the blind desire in him that made him want to paint.

He had worked himself into a good humour, and seemed to grow mellow and expansive, as if something had been loosened in him. His talk was strange, and listening to it I admired him without knowing why. He was telling me about an office job he had held for a short time in his youth, when he had been my age, and was about to become a renegade.

"One morning I was full of ideas for a wall painting. I was like you in those days, lad—inspired. Wish to God I felt like it now. There I was, with ideas pouring into my head in a steady stream. I couldn't sit still. Half of them I lost because I couldn't get 'em down quick enough. I was sketching away like a madman on bits of scrap paper, watching the boss out of one eye and my colleagues out of the other. That was when I was young, lad!"

I laughed. "What happened?" I asked, not wanting him to stop.

"I did what I always used to do—retreated to the lavatory. A wonderful thing, the privacy of the lavatory. Only I daren't stay there too long, or they got suspicious and asked awkward questions. The trouble was, I lost track of time in that place. I sat perched on my throne with a wad of paper, surrounded by all the pornography, dashing down the bones of a masterpiece. What an atmosphere!

"Sometimes I got panicky, when it was really quiet; I thought the sound of the pencil scratching on the paper could be heard all through the building. So I used to give the chain a yank, and have some covering activity. I can hear that water flushing away now—sweet music!"

"How long were you in that job?" I asked curiously.

"That one? Three weeks. Then they gave me the bullet."

He laughed hoarsely, exposing a mouthful of bad teeth.

"Don't let yourself be influenced by me, lad," he said. "I'm anti-social."

There was something fiery and inspired in his talk, yet he was a failure. I discovered this afterwards, but it was there, in his hunched shoulders, for me to see. That was why he talked, why he was afraid to stop. There was a void in him, and though he felt a power somewhere, he could never reach it or call it up. Ten years ago he had studied incessantly at art schools. As he told me about his life in London and elsewhere I became filled with a queer exultant feeling, and longed to have those experiences myself. It sounded mad and free. Though he missed out the squalor that he must have known, I doubt if that would have deterred me, even if he had stressed it.

It was hard to understand why he could not paint, when he thought of nothing else, and knew genuine from false. It was baffling. He could discriminate unerringly, and always reject the spurious, yet when he came to his own work this sense seemed to fail him. He couldn't make it wield a brush. There was a mysterious blind spot in him. When he came to speak about art theories he did not have the fire that ran through his other talk. He spoke like a man who has lost his way, and takes refuge in criticism. Everywhere in the room I saw evidence of his purposelessness, yet the slovenly disorder half fascinated me. After all, it was a kind of freedom, where nothing mattered. But was it a Bohemian existence, or the life of a failure?

Before I left, Cecil arranged another visit, so that he could give me my first lesson in composition. He was going to explain grouping and patterns to me. I was amused by this absurd mechanical approach of his, but agreed to come because I wanted to see him again, and hear him talk. And I was determined to maintain my foothold in this strange world, though I wasn't at all sure whether I belonged to it. But in its stale air I smelled a queer, thwarted, back-against-the-wall life, an impracticable, underworld existence, and that was irresistible.

We were at the door. Cecil seemed anxious to get back to his painting now.

"That's all you need, discipline," he kept saying, shutting the door an inch at a time. Then he opened it hastily to take my membership fee of ten shillings. I got on my bicycle and rode home, full of rebellion against everything.

vi

The following Saturday evening, when I knocked, there was no sign of life. After a long time I heard weary, dragging footsteps in the hall, and a woman I had never seen opened the door. She was Cecil's mother, an elderly creature with a thick round body, her head cocked slightly to listen. She wore a dark shiny dress and a grey woollen cardigan. From her neck dangled a heavy locket on a ribbon. She stood there on unsteady legs, staring, and for a moment I thought I had come to the wrong house, not able to connect her with Cecil, until she squeaked: "You the new member Cecil was telling me about?"

"That's right," I said.

"He said something about you coming. Well, he's not here. You'll find him down at the pub, I expect, bottom of the road."

And she shut the door.

It was getting dark when I reached the pub. Inside the atmosphere was so thick with smoke that I had difficulty in finding Cecil at first. Then I saw him in a corner. He had one arm around some woman in a fur coat who sat beside him. I felt sure he had seen me, but he gave no sign. I went over and placed myself in front of him, deliberately.

"Hallo, Cecil," I said.

Even then he kept his head ducked for a second. Then he looked up slowly, as if surprised.

"Eh? Oh, there you are, lad. Sit down here, by me. That's right, that's the idea. How are you, then?"

The forced politeness of this last question made me angry for an instant; then I saw how funny the situation was. After arranging my visit he had probably forgotten about it, and now he did not know what to do with me. He was already drunk, but it did not prevent him from being embarrassed. I sat there like a lump of stone, oblivious of his feelings. I guessed shrewdly that he was spending my ten shillings, if it had not gone already, and that gave me a right to be there.

When he saw that I had no intention of moving, he said, "Joan, I want you to meet our new member. You'll like his stuff. Strong, wild. He's got something, this boy. I'm going to teach him control; yes ... that's all he needs ... easy ... my methods, easy ..." and he broke off, swaying in his seat and mumbling. His eyes were narrow slits.

"Come on, come on," he mumbled to his companion. "Bugger 'em all."

He wanted her to empty her glass. She smiled her contempt at him. Then he surprised me by emerging from the fuddled depths and becoming very careful and exact in his speech, as drunks often are. Turning to me as he recovered, he said: "Joan doesn't paint, do you, Joan ... No. She's what you'd call an admirer. Yes, that's about it. Eh, Joan, old girl?"

The woman nodded curtly, without altering her rather cold, lecherous expression. She was plump, and had a white, bleak face. She wasn't drunk.

"That's right, Cecil," she said, and leaned across the table to me. "How did you know he was here?" she asked. "Did somebody send you?" I was chilled by her way of talking about him in the third person, and nodded. The woman rose to her feet at once.

"Somebody'll be here in a minute," she said calmly to Cecil. "You know that. There'll be another scene in here if you don't watch out." Then she smiled falsely at me and held out her hand. "Bye-bye, genius. Look after poor old Cecil, there's a good boy," she said, and went out.

"You'll have to excuse me," he was mumbling, as if to himself. "You'll have to," he moaned. "D'you hear me?" He was in his cups again, swaying to and fro, and as he swayed his head sank a little lower, towards the table.

"Yes, I hear you," I said.

Cecil made no reply. He became preoccupied with his empty glass, sliding it about childishly on the wet table-top. I sat beside him in the crowded, indifferent room, not knowing what to do.

Suddenly he raised his head, looking almost sharply at me. It was a remarkable recovery.

"Listen to me, young man," he said, solemn and heavy. "Don't rely on my promises, they don't mean anything. Understand? That's my temperament. It's how I am." And a little frown of pain appeared on his forehead. "I'm erratic, I say all kinds of things. I'm irresponsible—see? Oh, it makes me so ashamed!"

I laughed. "That's all right," I said.

"Don't laugh," he moaned. He put a large hand on my knee. "Listen, I'll tell you something now." He leaned sideways and began to whisper urgently, "I'm as tight as a drum—d'you know that? Have you noticed? Listen, I can't get home by myself, can I? It's impossible . . ."

"I'll walk down the road with you, when you're ready," I said.

"Will you?" he moaned. "Will you really?"

"Of course," I said, and grasped my opportunity. "Shall we go now?"

He stood up sleepily, like an obedient child, and I got him across the room and through the doorway without difficulty. He let me steer him through the people, and I felt there was something spectral about him as he leaned on my arm. He kept sinking away into his submerged, glowing world and rising again, like an unhappy fish.

Outside in the darkness he blundered against me, then staggered and almost fell into the hedge. He was whimpering now, as the cold air cleared his head a little, and he rose out of his drunkenness again. I had never been drunk myself, but I imagined how desolate he felt, having to face cold reality after the ancient, enveloping warmth he had just known.

"I'm no bloody good," he choked, as we wandered along. "Don't get mixed up with me, son, I'll only waste your bloody time . . . I can't paint . . . not now . . . I could once . . . I used to be bloody good, once . . ."

"You still can," I said earnestly, for I could not bear his despair. "You'll feel different in the morning." And in an attempt to cheer him up I added with conviction, for it was the truth: "I'm glad I've met you, Cecil!" and took his loose hand, shaking it vigorously.

He brightened up for a moment, lifting his weighted head and blinking happily.

"Any time," he muttered. "Come any time you like."

We had reached his house. I ran up the path and knocked on the door. Then I left him, outside the gate, holding on to the garden fence, because he refused to budge from that spot. He was muttering to himself about the shallowness of modern art, the need for a tradition, for roots, and suddenly he cried out in a loud voice that we had no giants like Michelangelo, we would never stand the test of time, we would all perish with the century. As I went down the road I heard the door open and his mother shout: "Cecil! Come on in, for God's sake!"

# *Four*

When I saw Cecil Luce again he looked depressed. He scowled as he let me in, though his greeting was friendly enough.

"How's life?" he said.

Once more there was no sign of his mother. The thought flitted through my head that he was out of work now, and that his mother had taken a job somewhere—despite what he had told me about Pearsons. Perhaps his mother really was a charwoman, I thought; that would explain her appearance. I had difficulty in imagining Cecil employed anywhere. He seemed too sluggish altogether.

I glanced round the room idly. Each time I came into it I told myself it was a studio, the first one I had seen, yet it remained a room. Somehow it was too familiar and suburban to be anything else.

Then I noticed a new painting. It stood out from the others because it was so unlike them. I stared at this head of a girl, youngish, with a mop of fair, springy hair.

"That's good," I said. It was really quite ordinary, but I was pleased with him for doing something other than brittle abstractions.

"Tell me what you make of it," he said casually. "I only did it the other day."

He sagged into a chair, watching me gloomily.

"Don't ask me to do that," I laughed. "I just like it."

He shrugged, fumbling for a cigarette.

"Who is she?" I asked. I kept looking at the long white neck, and almost asked him if it was really as long as that.

"Oh, she's a member," he answered. He rolled his unlighted cigarette around in his lips. "Jessie Hammond."

He went on to tell me that she lived in the suburbs somewhere,

53

and he banged his forehead slowly with his fist, trying to remember. It would not come. She had recently returned from North America. Not long after the war ended she had gone there to marry an American soldier, Victor Massarella, whom she met in Birmingham. Cecil remembered him, a short, dark fellow. Now she was divorced.

Just then the inner door opened and Cecil's brother came into the room. He had broad shoulders, and some taut, puckered skin around his mouth, on one side of his face. He came bursting in, but slowed down as he saw me.

"Oh, sorry," he said.

Cecil started to introduce us, then realised he had forgotten my name.

"Nick Chapman," I told him, smiling.

"Of course, of course," he said absently, without interest.

His brother was a strange contrast, very carefully dressed, with a fat, clean face, and a white cigarette in his mouth. He seemed to be examining me curiously. I was glad when he left.

ii

I went to one of the meetings of the group, which were held once a month in a room over a pub. Cecil took me there himself, leading the way along a stone-flagged passage and up a short flight of narrow stairs. It was the pub I had found him in a few Saturdays before.

The place was full of people, or seemed to be, and I felt bewildered. Yet I was grateful because no one looked up or stopped what they were doing. It was a fairly large room, with a square, recessed window at the far end of it, in the other short wall. On the floor were long strips of rather frayed coco-nut matting, colourless and dusty. The walls were whitewashed, with two heavy black beams overhead, along the ceiling, and the woodwork, door and window and skirting boards had all been painted bright yellow. Two long settees were placed together and ran along one wall, covered in worn rexine, and there were two gold-painted wicker armchairs. The wall opposite the settees only had a piano against it.

Two men and a woman were standing around the black fireless hearth, looking at a row of little terracotta figures on the broad mantelpiece. I recognised the woman's face almost at once from Cecil's picture, but he had made her younger than she was. She was about thirty.

Cecil stood gazing about in his dingy brown suit, evidently pleased at so large an attendance. His eyes took on a fixed glare of preoccupation behind the thick lenses and his voice grew soft and paternal as he told me that two or three of the group had decorated the room between them, and cleaned it up. Before it was almost uninhabitable, he explained. For years it had only been used for storing unwanted furniture.

As we loitered there, the fur-coated woman of that other evening came forward from somewhere; only now she had bare plump arms, and wore a taffeta dress of shiny dark grey, with bold slashes of white. She looked less vulgar in it than in the fur coat. She was even graceful as she stood coolly before Cecil, smiling a greeting at me. There was something frank and reckless about her that I could not help admiring.

"There you are, dear," she said.

"Hallo, hallo, Joan," Cecil said, and made as if to shamble off with her, his arm going automatically around her waist. Then he remembered me. He looked over his shoulder and leered, like a malevolent old tom-cat, just as he had done that night when he was drunk.

"Over here, lad," he said, and I felt his large hand grip my arm. "Come and meet Jessie." The three of us walked forward together, his hand pulling me gently to the other end of the room.

"Jessie, this is a young chap who's just joined us," Cecil began. He scratched his head. "Damn it, I've forgotten his name again."

The young woman threw back her head and laughed. "Oh, Cecil, you're hopeless!" she cried, but her eyes shone with warm affection. Joan was gazing pityingly at him.

"It's Nick," I offered.

"That's right, yes, that's right," Cecil said. "He's been admiring your portrait, Jess." And he leered at her in exactly the same debauched, tom-cat way, as though he could not help it. Joan dragged at his coat sleeve and he slouched off with her towards another gathering, so that I was left with Jessie and the two men who were with her. I did not know what to say.

"Hallo," the young woman said, laughing. "So you admire my picture. I *am* flattered."

For a few seconds I was horribly confused, and thought she meant that she had painted the picture herself. The two men were talking together in low voices. One was tall and thin, with a wispy moustache, and pale, jeering eyes. As he spoke he stroked the soft hairs on his upper lip with the tip of his finger.

"I thought it was a very good painting," I managed to say.

"Oh, is that all!" Jessie cried in mock disappointment. Her neck was very long, just as in the portrait. All the time I was ransacking my mind for something intelligent to say, but I only grinned and felt foolish. I felt sorry for her because she so obviously did not know what to do with me. The two men were still talking, though they had moved away from us now. They were an odd pair. The tall, thin one was leaning down to his companion confidentially. This other man, in a baggy grey suit, was like a man painted by Soutine. He was short, with a tiny, puckish face, brown and wrinkled like a pear, and reminded me at once of Francis, the little man who had collapsed in the park years ago. He stood there solemnly, sagging at the knees, catching the words his friend dropped down to him and nodding vigorous agreement.

"Do you paint?" I asked. I was ashamed of my rough voice. It was too loud, it sounded like a bellow.

"No, I'm an outcast. I'm the only one who doesn't, apart from Joan." Jessie's lips pouted, and she laughed. She was holding an apple in her right hand, and as I watched she raised it to her mouth and took a large bite. How red and shiny her lips were! I thought. She sank her teeth ravenously into the moist flesh of the fruit.

"You must think me awfully rude, but I haven't had any tea. I came straight here from work. I can't offer you one, I'm afraid. Would you like a bite?"

Her brown eyes sparkled with mischief. I was too startled to answer, and felt blood rush into my face. Because I had not spoken she began to wave the apple to and fro underneath my nose. It was stained pink with lipstick.

"No, thanks," I said at last.

Suddenly she was calm and serious.

"I do these things," she said, pointing to the row of figures along the mantelpiece.

They were like some Sardinian sculpture I had seen once in the Birmingham Museum. Most of them were figurines, not more than six inches high. They looked very old and atavistic, with their rough, stiff, earth-coloured bodies, and ceremonious gestures. I could hardly believe that this woman munching the apple had made them, with her neat modern hands. They might have been dug out of the ground, they had such an encrusted, ancient appearance.

A young man with a lot of loose black hair began to play the piano. The music flowed out easily, fluently, and seemed to calm the room. It was quieter now, though people still hung about, chattering. I noticed Joan, seated in one of the low wicker chairs, softly stroking her knees as she watched the pianist.

Gradually the long cascades of notes drew all the people closer. There were about a dozen. They drifted up slowly, as if the music was a fountain or a waterfall, and fascinated them. The settees filled up, and Jessie sat in the remaining chair. I found myself sitting next to Cecil. A young man near the piano had discovered a stool to sit on.

"That's Ted Braby," whispered Joan, leaning her head towards me and swivelling her eyes. "You'll soon get to know the names." She sank away again, her wicker chair creaking, before I had time to ask whom she meant; I supposed it was the pianist.

The man squatting on the stool suddenly produced a short wooden flute from his jacket pocket, making his eyes narrow and cunning, and then I heard Jessie say, in a low, pleading voice, "Norman—don't!"

He lifted his head, grinning.

"Don't what?" he said. His face was swarthy, with prominent cheek-bones. He sat very upright.

"Don't what?" he repeated.

I was watching Jessie and saw her change colour, with the eyes of the others on her. When she spoke again her voice shook a little with nervousness, and a thrill of sympathy went through me.

"Don't be a fool, and play that thing," she said.

Norman cocked his head to one side and closed his eyes, swaying slightly on his stool, like a snake-charmer.

"Play it, did you say?" he murmured, and raised the short pipe to his lips once more. This time he let out a swift burst of shrill music, cutting across the piano, and the pianist paused and turned on his seat, smiling, with his hands resting on the keys.

"Sorry, Ted," Norman said. He bent his head over the little shaft and played 'John Peel', giving the quick time an attractive off-beat rhythm of his own.

There was a burst of laughter, and some rain-drops of applause, when he ended. He scrambled to his feet and bowed, graceful and mocking, inclining his stiff back.

"Can't we have a duet?" he said to Ted Braby.

Everybody began to talk, and wander about. I wanted Norman to play the flute again. I could still hear the plaintive, mournful notes vibrating in the room.

Jessie came over and sat beside me.

"Did you like the Chopin?" she asked. She was dressed neatly in black; I thought she was probably a typist.

"No, not much," I answered boldly. I felt out of things, and it was making me angry.

"Oh! Why not?"

"Chopin was womanish," I said, with quiet contempt. Then my mouth began to tremble and I had to stiffen my lips.

"Don't you like women, then?" she asked in amusement, but with tolerance, as if she were quite used to dealing with abnormal people.

I grinned desperately. "We're talking about music," I answered rudely.

"Quite right, quite right!" cried Norman. He still sat obstinately on his stool. "Jessie, you're out of order."

"D'you mean that Chopin's sentimental?" asked Ted Brady from the piano. His long, glossy black hair flopped over his eyes and he kept pushing it back, his gaze fixed on my face.

"I don't know if he was or not," I said, "but that's how he makes me feel. I can feel my backbone melting away." I was growing more confident now, and began to glow with excitement.

"How do you like to feel?" cried Jessie. "I mean, why must you have a backbone?"

"If you haven't got one, you're a cripple," I said.

"But don't you admire his beauty—the beauty of the music? Surely you admit that? It *is* beautiful, you know." This was from Ted Braby, who had become agitated, running his fingers through his hair, a pale-faced, intense young man.

"Ask him if Beethoven meets with his approval," shouted the little man with the creased face, from near the doorway.

"What about the moderns, then?" demanded Ted urgently. I wanted to laugh because he was so serious, and had to get something settled at once. "What about Bartok, Sibelius, Stravinsky?" He fired off the names, then sat in intense expectation.

"Sibelius makes me feel like a god," I said. I was reckless and intoxicated with all the attention I was getting. I kept turning red, but I no longer cared.

"Put some on, put some on the gramophone!" chanted Joan. "Let's see what it makes him look like!"

Cecil Luce leaned back in the corner of one of the settees, putting a cigarette to his thick lips and blowing smoke down his nose. He was eclipsed for the moment. Music meant nothing to him. There was only one art, painting. All else was incomprehensible.

I waited in readiness for more questions. None came. I was not expansive enough, and they had lost interest in me. Really I was relieved, though there was a faint tinge of resentment.

I wondered why there were no paintings on the walls, which looked strangely bare. Then I noticed a stack of canvases in a corner, piled carelessly, with frames of all sizes and colours.

After a time the whirl of talk swung round of its own accord to the purpose of the meeting, which was the arrangement of the forthcoming summer exhibition. We all gathered around Cecil now. He sat back and glared blindly at us, dropping ash over the brown cloth of his trousers. I looked at his face in wonder, at the sightless, abstract ferocity of his expression. He glared around, turning the fierce heat on us all, intense and paternal, until we fused together into his 'group'. That was what he was up to. No wonder he forgot names, I thought.

It was agreed that one of my water-colours, a street scene,

should be hung, and Ted Braby offered to lend me a frame. My name was to appear on the catalogue, and for a few minutes I felt very puffed-up and important.

I watched Jessie as Cecil was mouthing out these arrangements and saw how eagerly she listened. Clearly she respected and admired him. She sat forward in her pleated dress, hanging on to every word. I stared at her white throat and lightly flushed cheeks, and could not believe she had been married.

It was over, and the meeting began to break up.

"Come over here," called Ted Braby to me. He was standing by the pile of paintings in the corner, holding up one of the smaller canvases. "Let's have your judgement on this."

"We'll come as well!" cried Jessie, leaping up and grasping Norman's arm, and they were the first to reach the other man.

"This one," Ted Braby said, pushing back the wing of black hair which seemed to torment him. He poked a lean finger at the picture he had propped against wall, on the floor. "Don't be afraid to say it's rotten, if that's what you think," he said, and laughed abruptly, a short high peal, tilting his long chin.

"Rotten," said Jessie with a straight face, and Norman aimed a kick at her.

The painting was in one of the modern French styles, something like Buffet, though his name was unknown to me then. It showed a young man in a bare room, seated on a chair. The bare floorboards sloped up oddly, with deliberate faulty perspective, lifting the figure out of the picture. Everything was grey and stony and impoverished, without hope, and cruel with truth. It made me wince.

"It's good," I said, biting my lip.

"Any criticisms?" asked Ted anxiously. He was disappointed. "You're letting me off too lightly, it's not good for me."

I looked again, trying to force my thoughts to the surface.

"It gives me the feeling that you're ... I don't know ... trying to suffer," I said. It sounded ridiculous, but it was too late to recall it now.

"You mean self-conscious?" Norman said softly, just behind me. I was startled; my shoulders jumped violently. He had spoken into my ear.

"Yes." The word flew out of my mouth before I could stop it. I meant nothing of the sort.

We talked on about the picture, and from that to the latest fashions in art, the most recent trends, the swings this way and that, the veering away from abstraction by the French School, all of which was new and fascinating to me. I was hopelessly out of date with my information, but somehow I managed to hold my own. As we stood there, the painting of Ted Braby's grew in impressiveness for me. Its very silence and austerity was growing in power, I thought, and I felt astonished that this bemused, ineffectual-looking pianist should have accomplished it. He was in fact a dance-band pianist, and an ex-university man.

Jessie and Norman wandered away together, and I was left with him. I spoke of my own attempts and struggles. He listened respectfully, as I tried to explain the new version of realism, deepened and broadened, that I longed for, and the new feeling I wanted, like a grasping of hands which had known dreadful things, in the darkness. I told him it had to be a feeling bigger than any of the narrow, selfish ones we knew, bigger than family love, bigger than conjugal love, a fraternity which looked outside and beyond itself, and grasped hands involuntarily, in a sort of gratitude. I knew I had strayed and become incoherent, and was out of the realm of art, but I could not stop. And it amazed me, hearing my own voice rising and falling without a pause, as though intoxicated with itself. Was I ever that dumb-struck boy who used to sit imprisoned in ferocious silences, who made everybody in a room uneasy, the boy tortured by shyness, who longed to speak and dance and laugh, and dazzle them all?

### iii

I wanted to escape from Woodfield now. Getting to know Cecil Luce and the others finally decided me. I wanted something bigger and bolder, and Woodfield cramped me. It was not Birmingham, and it was not a suburb exactly. I felt nowhere.

Cecil's influence did not unsettle me, for I had been unsettled long before I met him. Reading about Jude Fawley in Hardy's book I thought instantly of myself, and for his Christminster I substituted London. The provincial dream was upon me, with London as its magic centre, drawing me to it. Perhaps meeting Cecil was something I needed to do, a last thing, I thought afterwards. I felt he had struck off my invisible chains, unknowingly, and I was free to go.

I had finished my apprenticeship two years before. At home things were little changed. My sister, who was a schoolgirl now, had replaced me as my grandfather's companion. She went with him on his Saturday shopping trips, and once a month he took her to the Hippodrome as a special treat.

Though the old man had retired again, a faint acid smell still clung to him. There were particles of the white cadmium dust under his nails, caked hard and turning yellow. My mother did not expect him to live much longer, because of the diabetes, but I could see no signs of weakness yet. He was slower, and took a long time to get up, and that was all. He ate as well as ever, wiping his big moustache on his shirt-sleeve afterwards. When he tipped hot tea into his saucer and blew on it, he held the saucer with a steady hand.

"He's getting senile," my mother said, every so often. But I refused to believe it. If he was slowly dying, where were the signs? No, he was as lively as ever, and would go on and on. I imagined him outliving us all; it did not seem fantastic. He came from a robust age, and enjoyed life to the full. It never occurred to him to question it. For me he represented the past; my childhood, and before that, the childhood of my father. He stretched back like a bridge into the last century. Yet he was not grand or impressive. He was selfish. His dark eyes were watchful and bloodshot, still greedy for life, and his feet were firmly planted on the floor, as he stared out of his deafness at us. Sometimes I found it hard to regard him as my grandfather alone. It seemed presumptuous to think that. He sat in our house like a symbol for something, and I felt that he was the past, and belonged to everybody, like Warwick Castle.

# Five

## i

At the factory I handed in my notice, then waited impatiently for my last day to arrive. But when it came I was sorry to leave. Instead of the delicious feeling of escape I had expected, I faltered and almost turned back, not wanting to break with them all. I had tried to leave once before, and at the last moment cancelled my resignation. This time it was too late for anything like that. I wrenched myself out grimly, forcing myself to remember the monotony which had begun to crush and hammer me into a tool like all the others. I could not allow that to happen. So I turned my back on the whole eight years, confused and half frightened by the sheer madness of it. Everyone had called me a mad young fool, and I tightened my lips and said nothing. I had no plans. To prevent any future reversal I had even sold my tools and torn up my papers of apprenticeship. Then I walked through the gates for the last time, hardly knowing myself why I had done it.

There was still the ordeal of leaving home to face. I dreaded that as it approached. My mother watched my preparations grimly, yet in silence, and I had expected her to make some move to detain me. I knew it was not the fact of my leaving home which twisted so cruelly in her, but that I was going alone, without friends or even an address. To her the world beyond her family circle was a desert, a grim wilderness where homeless people wandered about, filling the cinemas on Sundays.

On the Tuesday of my departure I left her standing on the step, staring after me. Her small figure was perfectly motionless, as though frozen, and I could not bear to look at her. She was trying hard not to make a scene. I tramped on down the street with my bulky suitcase, not pausing or waving until I reached the corner. Looking back then, I was shocked to find her gone. The door of the house was shut, horribly blank, as if it had never been open to me. Panic whirled up inside me, then sank away, as I went on mechanically.

An hour later I sat in the express. It was taking a long time to get clear of the maze of points, threading its way through. As we went over a viaduct, high above the streets, the steel construction grumbled and howled under the loaded wheels. It was always the same on this section; it happened five minutes after leaving the station. Below were the roofs and chimneys, and a dense jungle of brick, with straight narrow channels cut through for streets. I gazed down dreamily, and then a mass of intricate girder-work blocked the view.

We were rushing headlong towards London. Suddenly I felt helpless before this fate which had put me here, which was hurling me forward and guiding the rails like cruel rays into the very heart of the city. The train tore through all the wayside stations without stopping once, sucking scraps of paper into the air, whirling them aloft like dead leaves, and I saw the faces of waiting people screwed up convulsively in a vain attempt to ward off the sudden violence, as the rocking coaches swept past them.

I was trembling inside, fearful and anxious, yet at the same time I felt vividly eager for any experience. If I lived very cheaply I could last out for months without a job. London was a vastness I had longed for, something that I hoped would absorb me and make me nameless for a while. I thought naïvely that if I made myself free of the past, a new life would somehow begin for me. It was all very vague and impracticable, but not impulsive, as everybody thought. I always brooded over a thing for a long time before I acted.

In my suitcase lay a large rolled-up water colour, painted on a sheet of cartridge paper, which I had brought as an example of my work. This was my masterpiece; I had spent three weeks of evenings on it, slaving over the design night after night in that tiny box-room where I slept. Once I even got out very early in the morning in my pyjamas and switched on the light, so that I could make a minute alteration. I tiptoed about the room with bare feet because the silence of the house was so deathly. As I stood shivering, admiring it, turning it different ways on the drawing-board, I kept telling myself it was magnificent, that I must have been inspired or insane to have concocted such a monster. It was certainly weird. I turned it upside down and refastened it, then climbed back into bed and looked at it again. The swelling legs of the bodies waved in the air like trees growing out of the floorboards.

Finally, when I got out and returned it to its correct position, I grew critical, and began to wish I had left them all standing on their heads. The forms were more mysterious that way. It was a picture of five figures, some of them huge, crowded into a room. I think they were dancing, and at the same time trying to burst out of the room, to escape. As I examined it coldly, I saw bold hints of Picasso and Max Beckman. Chagall must have been there too; I had a passion for him then. Perhaps that was his presence at work in the bottom left-hand corner, where a wine bottle danced nostalgically and the table floated like a cloud. The reeling, purple-brown figures seemed to be original, until I saw Henry Moore plainly in the heads, which were as small and calm as turtles, with long chalky Egyptian noses. And those eyes in the middle of the picture, glowing like great soft flowers behind the spokes of an orange cartwheel, must have owed something to Rousseau. Yet somehow it remained mine, in spite of the influences. It was my idea to have life bursting from a room.

The train was entering London, slowing down, and something began to grind and squeal. I watched the backs of houses slide past, all identical, mile after mile, the bricks dirty with soot. It was raining slightly. The man opposite me in the carriage was still asleep, his newspaper slowly slipping to the floor. He had twisted into a queer position. His long mouth was like a slit in his yellow face.

A big man against the window stood up to drag a suitcase from the rack, the flesh of his neck bulging over his collar. His large back seemed to fill the carriage. Suddenly the train halted, all the carriages crashed together, and the big man staggered and clutched the rack. "Blast!" he muttered, gasping for breath. All his neck was dark red.

We had reached Euston. I got out and wandered up the platform in search of the buffet, my suitcase banging rhythmically against my leg. The place was crowded when I found it, just after six, so I had to drink my cup of tea standing against the long counter.

It seemed strange being away from home. I was free. So this was London! I thought, and laughed to myself. It was so ridiculously easy to escape. The railway was like a magic carpet, it would take you anywhere. Home was a hundred miles away. I had nowhere to stay for the night, but I refused to think about it yet; there was plenty of time. I looked round at the dense crowd drinking and eating, chattering together, sitting in little groups around the small tables. Then I thought of the factory, and grinned triumphantly. The dull eyes of the waitress seemed fixed on me, and I felt suddenly raw and provincial. Feeling foolish, I asked for a piece of cake. But what did it matter? What did anything matter now? None of these people knew me, and that was what I wanted.

ii

A policeman told me I would find cheap lodgings at Lomas Street, near Victoria Station. I had come out of a tube entrance on the Embankment just as a train was gliding smoothly across the river like a brilliant snake in the darkness.

It was drizzling when I got there. I wiped my face dry with a handkerchief, straining to read the high nameplate of the badly lit street. It was a squalid little side street, so dismal and callous-looking that I almost turned away; but there was no time left to look anywhere else.

I walked down it, and passed a cart-horse standing in the gutter. It stood very still and hung its head, harnessed to a large cart. Somehow it seemed fantastic to come upon a horse in the centre of London. Its crinkled skin under the street lamp was a bluish colour. Steam rose slowly from its sides.

In Lomas Street there was a youth hostel, and, farther on, a place called the Charles Guest House, which turned out to be a hostel for working men. I did not know which of these the policeman had meant.

Nearby I heard a clock whirring hard to produce ten nervous strokes, and before it ceased Big Ben started to crash out majestically, like a master correcting his too eager pupil. Sound billowed in great waves over my head and died away. The charged interval between each mountain of sound thrilled me, as the whole night quivered and became a dark body, vast and unknown and ritualistic.

I crossed the deserted street which gleamed black with rain under the lamps, and mounted the steps of the Guest House. Inside there was a square opening cut in the blotchy inner wall, and a man with a thin hollow face sat behind a wire grill, at a cash register. He had a wide ginger moustache with spiked ends, and sat there importantly, stiff and ceremonious.

"Yes?" he rapped out at once. He had not even raised his head.

"Can I stay here for the night?" I asked, in a careful voice.

"Full up."

He had looked up briefly. Now he was bending over some papers. Behind him I could see a big kitchen, and two busy men in greasy aprons, their arms bare. One was tattooed heavily on both his arms.

"You haven't got any room at all?" I asked involuntarily.

The man lifted his head at this like an angry dog, his eyes gleaming.

"What?" he said. "We can't very well have room, can we, if we're full up."

He smirked then, relishing his own sarcasm, and I wanted to spit in the emaciated face behind the wire. I turned away to pick up my suitcase, hot with anger and humiliation, and suddenly the man said, "Wait a minute. There's one bed, in room C."

"Oh. I'll have that, then."

The official began to jerk out short, martial sentences. "It's only a small room, only twelve beds. It's clean. Not noisy. It's got a carpet. Nice room. Bed number nine."

He made an entry in a large register.

"One and six. Breakfast?"

"Yes," I said.

"Two and six."

As I handed over the money he muttered a few directions, pointing to a door on my left. I went through into a small, smoke-filled room. It was like a den. Men were sitting about at bare trestle tables, reading newspapers and playing cards. An incongruous, cultured voice droned out from an old radio shaped like a beehive, perched on a high shelf. No one took any notice of me. One man was asleep, his head pillowed on his arms, near a heap of dominoes. Looking round, bewildered, I saw a narrow doorless opening in the opposite wall, under the radio, and above it a down-pointing finger had been painted, with the inscription: 'Bedrooms C, D, E'.

Going across to it, I found myself at the bottom of a flight of stone steps, worn hollow and uneven. There was an iron banister sloping upwards, roughened by corrosion. A choking smell of dust hung in the air. I climbed two short flights of steps and came to my room. As I entered, a powerful smell of disinfectant met me, and I forgot the other smell. The room was empty, so I put down the heavy suitcase and stared around nervously. The yellow walls were discoloured and stained with dampness, but everywhere was in dark shadow because of the dim light.

Two rows of beds faced each other, like a hospital ward, with wooden fences between each pair of beds, about the height of a man, as a sort of grudging concession to privacy. I looked for my bed number, and found it eventually. Then I lifted my suitcase on to the bed and sat down beside it, gingerly. The silence was uncanny. Everything seemed grey and blurred, unbelievably dreary, but I was too tired to feel depressed. I kept reminding myself that I was in London, sitting on a bed in the very heart of London. It was all unreal.

I unfastened the suitcase and began to unpack a few things. Suddenly the pleased, triumphant feeling came over me, and I slammed my fist into the pillow. It did not matter, I had the place to myself. I even chuckled aloud, feeling my eyes flash with triumph at what I had done.

When I had undressed and slid the suitcase under the bed, I turned back the sheets and climbed in. I felt grimy, but did not know where to wash, and there was no one to ask. My legs and shoulders ached, though in myself I no longer felt tired. I was wide awake, and curious to see who slept in this room. I lay on my back and waited, hearing somebody climbing the stairs. The footsteps went past the door and started labouring up the next flight. But the silence was broken now. I could hear someone coughing in another room, and a person talking in a loud voice full of complaint. Still no one entered my room.

I opened my eyes, a sudden panic clutched me. Where was I? Then I remembered, and realised that I must have fallen asleep. Shadowy figures were moving about in the room, and I inclined my head slightly, to watch them without attracting attention. A man passed by the foot of my bed and disappeared through the inner door leading to the next bedroom. I could hear water running and splashing somewhere. Then I rolled over, my face turned towards the wooden screen, because two men were talking behind it in low voices and I wanted to listen to their conversation.

"Yes," said a grave voice, slowly. "Yes. I could tell you something about dancing. There are dancers and dancers. I saw the champions of Britain once. I used to be mad on it. I took lessons for three years, when I was a kid. Three years, and I never missed once."

"Fancy that," the other man said. His voice was full of awe and respect.

"I used to go to every dance there was. I never missed one."

"Go on!" exclaimed the other man. "You took it seriously, then? You studied it. You set out to master it."

"That's quite correct. I was mad on it. It got into my blood. It was nothing but dancing with me. I lived for it. Women didn't interest me, only as partners. It was all dancing, Pat. Dancing, dancing, dancing."

"Well! I've heard of that, you know. It got such a hold on you that you couldn't stop. Would you believe it!"

"Ah yes."

There was a pause, and the sound of a shoe falling loose from a foot.

"Like a craze," the encouraging, deferential voice said. "I've heard of that, yes."

"I went to a dance in Victoria Street the other week. I was dancing with a young girl. Slim, she was, with long black hair. Dolores type. And she was good; she could really dance. I could tell that in a minute. This one was different."

"I see what you mean! You'd notice the difference straight away, of course you would. It's an instinct with you."

"She said to me, 'You're a very good dancer.' I said. 'So you are.' She told me, later on that night, that I was the best . . . the best partner . . . she had ever had . . . to dance with."

"Is that a fact! And why not? She was telling the truth. She was grateful to you."

"Yes. Then suddenly . . . the man on the trumpet . . . played a wrong note. Just one. He fumbled it. And that finished me. I told the girl I was sorry, but I couldn't dance any more."

There was another dead pause.

"Do you know," said the grave voice, "that wrong note played on the trumpet . . . ruined my night's pleasure. And that's a fact."

"Just fancy! A wrong note! I can believe it. Oh yes. It upset your balance, it put you off. You were used to everything being first-rate . . . It jarred on your nerves, naturally."

I smiled to myself in the darkness. The story-teller became even more solemn and deliberate in his speech, pausing with great care for effect.

"There is only one . . . really . . . great . . . trumpet player. One. And that is Harry James."

"I've heard his name, yes," came the voice, warm with deference.

"The greatest trumpet player . . . in the world. It is marvellous, marvellous to listen to. He plays like an angel, that man. Without any effort. His tone is the most beautiful tone I have ever heard. Pat, that man is a born musician."

"Is that a fact, now!"

"Yes."

Then the dim light went out. It made little difference, and I hardly noticed. Somebody swore.

"They're early tonight, aren't they?" Pat's voice asked.

"Fifteen minutes," said his companion. "Bloody misers. See you tomorrow, Pat, my lad."

"That was a very interesting conversation!"

"I could go on all night," replied the other man. "But some other time."

I lay on my back with my eyes open. I was curious about the

two men, wondering what their faces were like. The air in the room was stale, and in it hung the sickly odour of disinfectant, mingled with smells of dampness and sweat. The man in the bed opposite had propped himself up and was smoking a cigarette. I saw it glowing strongly whenever he drew on it. It gave an odd touch of luxury and leisure to the mean room. Someone was mumbling to himself somewhere nearby, and I tried to trace the sound. It seemed to come from the bed next to the man smoking. Or was it farther to the left? I gave it up. I heard the word 'luck' repeated several times. In the darkness all around me, men were beginning to snore and breathe heavily.

I fell asleep, and dreamed I was in an enormous factory which had only one door. I could not find this door; I wanted to get out, at first calmly, then with an urgent need surging through my limbs. The great shed was full of acrid smoke. I kept rubbing my eyes and looking along a wall which stretched away into the distance. I ran past rows of screeching machines. Halting by one of the operators I asked the way, shouting at his head. The man did not hear. He bent lower over the machine, his face bathed in a pale greenish light. I wandered on for a long time, seeking this door. By an open furnace I suddenly clapped both hands to my face, saying: "Oh! It's hot! It hurts me!" Yet I had not felt pain. I felt my hair crackle with the intense heat, and fled. Then I came to where a massive steel hammer crashed down from the roof. It barred my way. Each time it fell a huge flame shot upwards like a column. I sat down on a wooden box and began to cry, and the tears splashed into the iron dust at my feet.

iii

I stood on the top steps of the hostel, buttoning my raincoat. A loose, heavy rain was falling, full of large soft drops. I had swallowed the unappetising breakfast and greasy tea as quickly as possible. A man was already standing on the steps when I came out and I glanced at him automatically. His face was raw and pulpy, as though battered by the weather. His brown eyes had a fixed, vacant expression. I was fascinated by a nerve which kept twitching in his cheek as he stood there holding the morning paper.

I looked along the street. In the darkness there had been something sinister about it; now it was only squalid, with its weary, insulted nakedness. On the other side, a little farther down, was a public lavatory, and next to that a large blackened building, three-storeyed, belonging to a scrap-metal merchant. A huge blue sign made of tin carried these three words above the first row of windows. One of the lower windows had a hole in it which had been blocked with cardboard. The grimy walls rose straight up to the roof, with no window-sills under the windows, like the walls of a factory.

A cat came out of an entry and ran across the street, disappearing through a yard entrance. The man beside me on the steps poked his head cautiously into the street and looked both ways.

"Miserable day," he said, staring vacantly at the opposite wall. He was a short, stocky man, and I noticed a large shiny boil on the back of his neck. I was beginning to feel chilly, though it was only September.

"Yes," I answered. "Yes, it is."

"I hope it stops soon. Blasted nuisance. D'you know what time they open the Out-Patients at St. Thomas's? I've got to go and see 'em before starting work."

"No," I said. "I'm afraid I've no idea."

The man thrust his hands into his trousers pockets. He did not have a raincoat, apparently. He wore a blue serge suit, which drew attention to his dirty white shirt. He stared moodily down at the pavement.

"I think it's nine. I hope so. It's my nerves," he said, and glanced into my face. "Nervous breakdown. I was discharged from the Army for it, or I'd be there now. I was in Germany two years."

"Oh yes." Then I said the first thing that entered my head. "Did you live in London before you went in the Army?"

"No, Ireland." He smiled wistfully; then his head shot round. "You a Londoner, mate?"

I grinned. It was pleasant to be asked that. "No," I answered, shaking my head. "No, not me." Couldn't he tell by my accent? I thought: that was before I realised that I had asked almost the same question. He did not sound like an Irishman. Whatever he was, I was glad he had spoken. I was grateful for someone to talk to.

"They don't like you, do they, the Londoners," he went on. "D'you think they do? I don't think so. No, they don't like foreigners here."

He shook his head sadly, gazing down fixedly at his shoes. It felt strange to be coupled with this man as a 'foreigner'.

"It's miserable, this place," he said, "when you're on your own. Isn't it? It's rotten. No brothers and sisters. I think it is, anyway. I don't like it."

Suddenly he stuck his hand into the street, like a beggar.

"I wish this rain'd stop. Bloody stuff." He fell silent for a moment; then I heard him say, almost to himself: "Any idea where the nearest Labour Exchange is?"

I shook my head again. "Sorry, I haven't." I felt rather stupid, and ashamed at being ignorant of such a fundamental thing. "Somebody inside is bound to know," I added lamely.

"Doesn't matter. It can wait."

We stood together, and I let my eyes wander along the street. A red postal van was coming quickly towards us, splashing through puddles.

I wore a raincoat and could have gone at once. But something made me wait for this man. There was plenty of time; I had nothing else to do.

The door behind us swung open and the warden came out. He was the man who sat behind the grille. His long face was sour with irritation. He wore a grey suit decorated with grease spots and was jingling loose coins in one of his pockets.

"Now then, you men," he said testily, "you don't have to stand on the steps. They'll think this is a common doss-house instead of a respectable establishment, if you hang about on the steps like that."

I stepped on to the pavement and began to walk casually down the street, trying to look as unconcerned as possible. I hated that man.

"I'll come with you!" cried the little man, and he jumped down and ran after me, quick and boyish. He trotted along by my side. The rain poured down, splintered on his bare head and started to run into his collar. He turned up the narrow collar of his jacket and hunched his shoulders.

"What does he think it is, the Savoy?" he cried angrily. "Dozy old bastard!"

I grinned sympathy down at him. "Not very friendly, is he?"

We went past the youth hostel, under its windows like flat glistening eyes.

"What harm were we doing, anyway?" cried the little man. His coat was sodden already, and every few yards he swore loudly. "What harm were we doing him?" he demanded again and again. He could hardly contain himself.

As we hurried along his anger subsided, as if quenched by the rain. Water trickled down his face, running off the end of his nose. He shook his head like a dog to get the water out of his hair, and lapsed into silence. Then he began to tell me of an episode he had witnessed about a week ago. It was in all the papers, he said. A man had jumped in the river from Westminster Bridge. He was drunk. He had been walking over the bridge; then he had turned and struck his wife and she fell on the pavement. He climbed on the parapet and jumped off the bridge, striking his head on something as he plunged through the water. He was pulled out with his face covered with blood, and afterwards sent to prison.

At the next crossing we parted, and that was the last I saw of my companion. I pictured him in a hospital waiting-room, sitting for hours in his wet jacket and with the nerve twitching in his cheek.

I had swung to the right, for the man's story had given me a sudden desire to see the river. The rain was easing off now. I did not know where I was, and then I came out at Millbank, near the Tate Gallery. As I neared the water I felt the air grow much colder. I reached the wall and leaned against it, resting my arms on the broad stone. A dense mist lay on the river, which looked cold and powerless, inert. I could only dimly see the shapes of buildings looming up on the far bank. The tide was out, leaving long stretches of rounded mud. A lovely feeling of freedom went through me as I looked down at the smooth mud and realised again where I was. Then I shivered, smelling the mist in my nostrils as it rolled forward.

A man was wading in the river, wearing rubber boots. He was holding a circular object, like a sieve, and hung his small bullet head over it. He made slow, methodical, curving movements with his arms, his hands out of sight, submerged in the grey oily water. Every so often he retraced his steps and went over to a bucket, emptying the sieve of its contents. He waded slowly back into the shallow water and began again, changing his position from time to time, working gradually towards the bridge. He had very square shoulders. I watched him for about ten minutes, until he was much farther away. A tug came by, belching out black smoke, hauling two broad barges which were low in the water. As I stood there a negro leaned forward against the wall, a few yards to my left. I had not heard him come up. His serious young face was wistful and north-bitten, reminding me of the negro circus performers in Picasso's early pictures. I felt sorry for him in his clean white collar. It gave him an imprisoned look, and made me think of an unhappy animal.

iv

At the hostel in Lomas Street, the warden was hated and feared. For some reason he was called the Captain. It may have been a nickname, or some rank invented for him by the owners, or perhaps he had really been a captain in one of the wars. I never found out.

Nobody hated him more than Dick Clewley. This man had a large, loose mouth, hanging open a little, and an oily skin. The tip of his nose was flattened, with nostrils which seemed to spread over half his face. He had a habit of loudly sucking his lower lip before he began to speak. It was like a warning. No one knew why he had such a hatred of the Captain, but he had been at this hostel for nearly three years; that in itself was a good reason, and something of a record. He was the first in bed every night in my room and would talk from there, sitting up and gazing around arrogantly, like a veteran patient in a hospital, his hands behind his head.

The Captain went clumping through all the rooms at seven each morning, waking everybody by blowing an outsize whistle.

He produced this harsh police noise with relish, jerking his elbow violently. All his frustration and malice went into it. One of the rules stated that the hostel must be empty by eight-thirty, so at eight the violent whistle was heard again, shrilling this time for the benefit of a few unemployed men who always refused to budge.

I had been there almost a week. Each night when I came in I asked myself why I did not find a cheap furnished room somewhere, so that I could have a little privacy. Yet, apart from the cheapness, it was difficult to give up my companions at this place, though they were illiterate and poverty-stricken, and I had made no friends. They were better than my own company. A room to myself was a bleak prospect.

On Friday night I was lying asleep, my head almost under the sheets, when a sudden yell terrified me. I thought I was dreaming. I found myself sitting up; then there was a loud crash. It was too dark to see anything.

Somebody yelled: "Get back into bed, you old sod!"

"What was that?"

"Jesus!"

"Noisy bleeder!"

The voices came from all directions. I could see a vague black shape moving about at the other side of the room. Then slowly my eyes became accustomed to the darkness. A man was sitting on the edge of the bed, a small, lively fellow called Yorky, who slept opposite me. I had noticed him smoking on my first night there.

"S'orl right, s'orl right," he muttered. "Nightmare . . . fell out of bed . . . quite all right . . . could have happened to anybody . . ."

He lit a cigarette. It glowed brightly in the dark room. He let out his breath in a huge sigh.

"Bloody hell," he said, in a quiet serious voice.

"For Christ's sake—can't you cut the cackle?" somebody shouted.

The bed creaked loudly. Yorky was scratching himself. He climbed back into bed.

"What time is it?" he piped.

"Nearly time to get up!" shouted the same furious voice.

I lay on my back, gazing up at the invisible ceiling. Somebody began to cough painfully. Another man had a peculiar snore which grated on the nerves, and I found myself listening for it against my will. I would never get back to sleep. The weird noise filled the room. It went into a choking sound, then a spluttering and grunting, before it began all over again.

Lying there I thought of the man Yorky, who had caused all the commotion. In the mornings he could never get up early enough. He groaned and sighed for a long time before he even sat up. Then he made a tremendous effort and got his legs out of the bed. Sitting like that, his pallid legs dangling, he would wait for another burst of energy to possess him. He would stagger to his feet with a rush and pull his trousers off the chair-back by the window, and drag them on, looping the braces over his shoulders, all in one rapid movement. He slept in his shirt. Under his bed he kept a battered wooden box with heavy hinges, and a great brass padlock hanging from the front of it. He was a wiry, energetic man, full of sprightliness when he was fully awake, with a high-pitched voice which rose to a squeak when he got excited. "Late again," he piped to himself every morning. "Oh dear, late again. This is getting a serious business!" I used to lie in bed and listen as he reprimanded himself.

He was a plumber's mate. It was a hard life. He seemed hardly suited for it, he was so perky and quick, like a music-hall artist. He came from the north, from Mansfield, and he had a mania for gambling. Horses, dogs, football: he followed them all. But it was mostly the dogs. He went off to the track most evenings. And the whole room would roar with laughter at his accounts of his misfortunes, when he returned and came up to bed, his small worn cap pulled jauntily over one eye. He would tell us about his bad luck, and what he was going to do to remedy this, looking round with lugubrious eyes. He believed passionately in luck.

"Ever since I started going to that laundry in Tunnel Road I've had bad luck!" he cried one night. "Ever since that day!" He leapt up. "I'm certain that's what it is, certain. I'm going to change that bloody place on Saturday, it's unlucky."

He fairly danced about the room, from bed to bed, growing more excited each minute.

He was always losing his cap. He would leave it hanging on the back of the chair or on the table in the dining-room downstairs.

"Oh dear. Anybody seen me cap?" he would ask. "I lost me cap."

"What's this? Is this it?" Somebody had brought it up. "You want to tie a piece of string on it," they told him, exchanging winks. And he rushed across to them.

"Ah yes! Thanks, mate."

One night when I came in early I found him sitting at a table under the dim yellow light, in the centre of the room. The light shedding on his head made his bald patch gleam. I wondered where he had managed to get the table. He must have dragged it upstairs somehow, I thought. Our bedroom was deserted, and there was no sound from the adjoining one. For the moment he had the place to himself. He was sitting in the yellow cotton shirt which he slept in and never seemed to change, sewing a patch on the seat of his trousers. His thin legs with wiry black hairs looked tough and muscular. Several toes poked out of his left sock. When I came in and went over to my own bed he did not notice, though I brushed against his table. He was utterly absorbed, working away intently in the circle of light. Occasionally he mumbled to himself. "That's right! That's better!" I heard him exclaim two or three times.

When he finally raised his head there were five men standing round him in a semi-circle. Dick Clewley was one.

"Oh!" he said, startled. The men were all grinning. They winked and exchanged sly glances.

Dick Clewley slapped his back and looked artfully at the others. "Is that where the dog got his teeth in?" he shouted. "You shouldn't go where you're not supposed to. You want to read those signs, Yorky."

"It's all right, it's all right," said the little man rapidly. "Just a few running repairs, that's all."

He was trying hard to thread the needle. He squinted up into the poor light and held the needle above his head, poking the cotton blindly at it. His head was cocked to one side. He swore, concentrating once more, and seemed to forget his critical audience. The men stood and roared with laughter. He was a comical sight as he sat there in his grubby yellow shirt, his bare legs tucked under the table.

# Six

## i

The weather had changed now, and an Indian summer began which lasted for over a month, well into October. Every morning was misty, and ripened gradually into a mellow warmth, until by midday I felt the blue heat weighing on my head.

I always hung back until the others had gone off to work, so that I could dress in private and have the wash-place to myself. On these fine days I got dressed quickly and often went out without breakfast, asking at the entrance if there were any letters. I had begun to hope for one from Cecil Luce, but it did not come. I would have been grateful for one from anybody.

There was a small area of garden at Millbank, with shrubs dotted about, rhododendron and privet, a rose tree, and a few seats, and I wandered towards it from the hostel, through the morning-fresh streets. I did this daily, as a sort of discipline. It was comforting to have a fixed point to aim at.

Sitting there I would read a letter from my mother, perhaps an old one, and watch the clerks and shop assistants rushing to work, pouring thickly along pavements and roads and over bridges. They were like hordes of insects, not people. As I stared I tingled all over with a delicious exultation, rejoicing in my freedom, my miraculous escape. Only a week or two ago I would have looked like that, I kept telling myself in amazement. It was like watching scenes from my past life. The river fog made me chilly, but I sat there until the swarm of traffic had lessened, and a young blind man with leathery lips came tapping towards me along the wall. He always appeared at nine, as the clocks were striking.

For the first few days I had done everything too fast. I read a letter, or glanced at a book, then stuffed it into my pocket hastily and almost leapt to my feet, ready to rush off somewhere. Even though I knew I had nowhere to go, I found it hard to remember.

And I had to force myself to walk slowly, adopting a deliberate measured stride, like a policeman's, among all the fever and excitement of everything rushing past me. How difficult it was to do nothing!

From Millbank each morning I used to walk towards Whitehall and Trafalgar Square, travelling on slowly up Charing Cross Road past all the bookshops. At one of them I found an old copy of Browne's *Religio Medici* buried in a heap of rubbish and bought it for sixpence. It was bound in tough, mustard-coloured covers, the pages made of thick coarse paper, and the print was black and heavy and substantial. It fitted easily in my jacket pocket, so I carried it about with me everywhere. One day I found the sentence in it which I had seen quoted somewhere years before, and my heart swelled again with the same pride and recognition and kinship. I chanted the words over to myself: "I have shaked hands with delight in my warm blood and canicular days."

I often saw the same men hanging about in front of those windows with nude photographs and dubious sex books on display, and I could not help pitying them. I knew what they were doing, but it was hopeless. It was like looking at another world through the bars of a cage.

In the same street was Zwemmer's, where I could gaze in at the Braque and Rouault colour reproductions for as long as I liked. I stared at the one Rouault many times, trying to commit to memory its tremendous simplicity and the rich organ notes of its colour. It was a small landscape.

Every morning I made the same pilgrimage. Occasionally, as I discovered new approaches, I varied my route a little. My ultimate destination was always Hyde Park. I used to try and time myself to reach there about noon, when the sun was at its hottest, the asphalt roads spongy with heat underfoot. It was like striking out for a raft which floated miraculously on the sea of noise and traffic, then crawling on to it and rolling on to my back. Once I arrived I just plopped down like everybody else, not caring where I drifted. I felt quite purposeless, without direction. Lying on that parched earth and withered grass in the September sun was a strange sensation, as if the whole swarming hive of London revolved round me like a crazy wheel, while I remained perfectly stationary; as though I lay over an axle which sank right down through earth and rock, and if I once moved away from that hub of stillness I would start spinning madly. I went quiet and drugged and vacant, as the sun baked me. When I moved I expected to creak like dry leather.

Sometimes I read a few pages of the book I had rescued, admiring Thomas Browne the man more and more as I grew aware of him behind those rolling, sonorous sentences of his. I would plough on blindly, not understanding, with the words I had read beating up like surf in my memory, thunderous and then quiet, rising and falling. Now and then I broke into clarity, and it was like emerging from a dark forest into the blaze of noon. In the midst of his pages I sensed a vast deep calm, a happiness, a power drawn from the middle of the sky. The solemn river of prose I was following would begin to laugh, forgetting that it was vast, and the air streamed with birds over my head. It was all calm and broad and inevitable, with sudden gloryings in the lust of the goat, or meditations on simple joys, a great rolling song tinted with death and rooted in contentment. The passages of pure theology were obscure, plunging me back into the forest. Then I read on for the impassioned language, the chords, letting the meaning float away like the smoke of a subterranean fire. It gave me intense pleasure to think of Thomas Browne sitting in his house at Norwich, perhaps at Christmas, crouched forward over a book, reading those pagan Greeks. I dwelt on it and tried to picture it all—his twelve children, his books, his tolerance, his canicular days.

ii

I dreaded the evenings, but while the daylight remained strong and the sun beat down, I knew I could defy the desolation. And being so utterly alone I had moments of pure happiness, in which my mind was as free of thoughts as the blue sky of clouds. I began to notice tiny things, to be absorbed by them, and I forgot where I was. I found myself looking at the pale dust on the blades of grass, the minute fissures in the baked earth, the drops of moisture glistening frostily on my skin. Raising my head a little I could see white buildings with exotic domes shimmering in the hazy distance, and it was easy to blot out the mean streets. It was only when the light weakened and the brown dusk gathered around the edges of this vast open ground, that I began to feel afraid. I scrambled hastily to my feet and made for the coffee-stall. There was a hum and a clatter of people there, and cheery talk, which heartened me. I stood listening to the bubbling and hissing of the gun-metal urn, and watched the small flames, white and blue, wavering and spurting underneath. On one side of me a shrunken man with a tooth-brush moustache sold evening papers, howling out forlornly, and almost at my feet against the railings a gipsyish pavement artist worked at his meticulous copies of old masters. His finest achievement seemed to be a large reproduction of the Laughing Cavalier, with all its intricate lace at the throat and wrists. It covered four paving stones completely, and the artist placed his dusty cap of money at the bottom of it.

From this spot I would head back into the maze of streets as the shops and offices were closing, and scores of people rushed out of buildings, running past me to form long queues for buses. It was the evening stampede, with everybody escaping from boredom with glad cries.

One evening as I walked away from the coffee-stall I glanced down into the basement of a big house, and saw a family seated round the table. The little room was warm with light. I could see their faces clearly, smiling and talking. Suddenly, as I loitered there, the whole scene became charged with anguish. The dying sun was flooding the street, bathing my hands and knees with its red death. Longing rose in my throat, and my eyes filled with tears. I hurried on, disgusted and frightened by this revelation of a weakness which I did not know how to fight.

I trudged past the row of big houses with my gaze averted; I did not want to see any more brightly lit rooms. But the one I had just seen kept returning; nothing would drive it away. I looked down again on the heads of the people sitting down to their evening meal. There was a man and a woman, and two boys. Some washing hung on a line over their heads. Then the scene faded, and a huge emptiness seemed to spread all over my body. It was like hunger. I felt exhausted. All the strength seemed to have poured out of me in a swift rush.

I came to a corner and stood helplessly. Passers-by cast curious glances at me. A couple walked by quickly, laughing happily.
They were lovers. The young man wore black pointed shoes
which were highly polished. His sleek dark head was bare, and
pressed down against the woman's hair, his arm encircling her
waist. Their laughter rang in my ears.

In desperation I changed direction a little and made straight
for the Westminster Library. It was good to hurry along like the
others and have somewhere definite to go. When I arrived it was
almost empty, because of the warmth and lateness. In twenty
minutes it would be closed. There were only two persons inside,
wandering about in silence. Something made me dart into the
reference section, and on a low shelf I found a bulky red volume
full of small reproductions of Van Gogh's work—more than I
had ever seen before. I went over to the dark treacle of one of the
tables with my treasure.

Dozens of the illustrations were of the Hague and Nuenen
periods. They were all black-and-white, but that only added to
their impressiveness. How different his solemn-faced peasants
were from Brueghel's, I thought. These early portrait heads were
carved out with deliberate crudity, stamped with melancholy,
suffering and labour. And I was amazed at the range of subjects,
never dreaming that he had cast his net so wide. He overlooked
nothing. It was almost terrible, this consuming desire to paint the
whole world. He had wanted everything for the huge, godless,
holy song he was going to sing. I sat gazing at these black biting
drawings and seething oil sketches, at Bibles, potatoes, apples,
flowers, birds, fish, mice, trees, birds' nests, cottages, books,
babies, horses, women, hospitals, fields, old boots, undergrowth,
the sea. It affected me deeply, turning the beautiful pages. I had
such a renewal of power that I forgot where I was, and I wanted
to grasp the hand of this dead man who was suddenly more
warm and living than the people about me. 'We do not lower him
with our pity,' I thought, 'yet pity is not enough to comprehend
his life, which must have known deep joy.'

Coming out in a daze, I turned to the right, starting to climb a
short hill. I was almost treading on the heels of a tramp, so I began
to pass him. He was a shrivelled, elderly creature, his brown face

covered with greyish stubble. He had a faded potato sack slung over his right shoulder. There were no heels in his socks. "Bloody horrors," he was shouting, in a weak voice choked with fury, "oh you bloody horrors," toiling on up the hill, and I wondered if he meant the incessant traffic or the people. I listened, slowing down to stay behind him, but he said no more.

It was getting dark rapidly now. On the other side of the street, on a corner, a large display window of some kind blazed with light, a bright yellow rectangle in the surrounding darkness. Shop blinds were drawn on either side of it. I began to walk across. There were tramlines in this street, shining under my feet. I reached the window, and looked in at the open newspapers propped up, and the enlarged texts displayed. It was a Christian Science reading-room. Inside, through the glass door, I could see a middle-aged woman with bare arms, seated at a narrow table made of pale wood. She was smiling at someone in the room while her hands fidgeted with a bowl of anemones in front of her.

I stood outside, not wanting to move away. The place was like a sanctuary of light and friendliness, beckoning me. I did not profess any religion, but this was not like a church, this bright room. Ordinarily I should have been contemptuous of the linking of science and ritual. I read one of the texts: 'Look unto Me and be saved'. And underneath that were the words: 'You have nothing to do but look and love'. It made me want to groan aloud. The words were like measured blows on my heart.

I swung away from the window and began to walk swiftly towards the West End, to find a cinema.

iii

The queue in Charing Cross Road was growing steadily. It curled round a corner and stretched halfway up a side street. I had been standing there for three-quarters of an hour, and no longer wanted to see a film. But it was still too early to go back to the hostel.

The doorman came out to survey the situation, taking off his green and gold cap and scratching his head. "'Strewth," he said softly, and ran down the queue.

"Come on, move up, move up there!" he shouted. "Get closer together, now. You'll be in the churchyard at the back there, if you don't close up!"

He smirked as though he had said something clever, twitching his sharp grey face. His eyes were like moist currants, watchful and fixed, over his pointed nose, and made me think of a rat.

A few minutes later he darted out of his hole again and came up to a young woman who was holding up the queue, preventing those behind from moving forward.

"Move up, close up," the doorman said, touching her arm.

She stood where she was.

"Can't you move up, love?" the man asked, leering at her.

"I'm saving somebody's place," the woman said crossly.

"What if they don't come back?" the uniformed man chanted, grinning round for approval. "You goin' to stand there all night?" Again he put a gloved hand on her arm. "Come on, now. Close up."

The woman turned red, then moved forward lumpishly without speaking.

"That's the idea!" cried the doorman. "Now we're getting somewhere!" And he scurried back along the gutter to the entrance.

In the main street the cars, buses and taxis ran past in an endless stream. A negro in a white felt hat walked over the crossing, at the mouth of the side street. Everything about him was soft and ripe, as if he were all pulp and blood. He wore a loose jacket with a loud check pattern, and his black skin under the drooping white trilby made several people in the queue look up, startled, and stare after him. I was fascinated by his slow padding gait, half waddle, half swagger, that was so soft-boned, so different to the others.

It began to spatter with rain, large ominous drops, the first rain for nearly a month, and one or two umbrellas went up. But most of the people were even without raincoats. The drops ceased and gave way to a thick drizzle. I watched the balls of moisture clinging and rolling on the greasy peak of a man's cap just in front of me. Then came a few minutes of quite fierce banging rain, and soon my hair was full of water.

I left the queue. My mind had been made up for me. I did not even know the name of the film.

People streamed past, all going in one direction, and I let myself drift along with them. I came to a corner and stood there a moment, then stepped off the pavement. Suddenly a tremendous voice bellowed in my ear: "D'you want to get killed?" The side of a red bus hung over me, towering up, and as it swayed past it brushed my shoulder. One of the giant rear wheels crunched against the kerb, only a fraction from my foot, as I leapt back. I stood trembling and watching it disappear.

The rain had eased off. Then it began again, and I started heading back for the hostel, from somewhere behind Bond Street.

I went past a number of shop doorways and saw women standing motionless in the shadows. Their lips and eyes glistened in the darkness. One stood near a street lamp, and I saw that she was tall, with reddish, piled-up hair, her face so heavily made up that it was like a crude mask. As I drew level she stared like a gipsy full at my face. My heart began to lurch about, beating wildly, and all at once my hands felt on fire. Mad, impossible thoughts filled my mind. I felt the insidious, inhuman potency lurking in the street, making it sinister. Though they were squalid, there was something old and inevitable about the waiting women, older than evil. In another age they would have been sacred prostitutes.

I sheltered in an empty doorway and waited, pretending to watch the rain. Did I want one of them to come up to me? I felt I was being tugged in several directions, my mind fogged with hot rushing thoughts. I tried to stand casually, and gazed up with all my will at the night sky, where it merged with the black of roofs. What if no one came up? I hoped they would not, yet at the same time I wanted something to happen, and the one rigid thing in this wavering was a refusal to give in to my fear. I stood with a strained, blank face, feeling that my reason for waiting there was obvious to everybody, revealed, like a placard hung round my neck. What would I say if anyone came? The thought made me tremble and want to run off. The street was absolutely deserted, yet I seemed to feel eyes watching me from every direction. I wish I had never submitted myself to this ordeal.

A car swung fatly round the corner, tyres swishing, lights smudging over the blue-black road. It crept forward obscenely like a black-beetle, and drew up not far from me, on the other side of the street, its engine purring. Inside, the driver's cigarette glowed mysteriously. Then a woman crossed over from one of the doorways, carrying an umbrella. The invisible driver slipped the catch of the door, in readiness. I watched the woman get in sedately, and the opulent car slide away from the kerb.

iv

A woman was advancing towards me. I had not noticed her because of the car. I stood rigidly. She wore a white plastic mackintosh, and stalked forward on long legs, holding an umbrella over her head of black shiny hair. She was smiling.

"Hallo, darling," she said, coming up to me, smiling. I stammered and could not speak, burning deeply with shame. Almost blindly I met her large black eyes, and the white, smiling face glowing out of the wet darkness. I struggled to speak, and a convulsion went through my body.

"Are you lonely, darling?" the woman said. She asked wearily, as if she did not expect an answer, with a foreign accent I was unable to identify. She stood closer to me.

"Would you like to come with me? You'd like that, wouldn't you? Have a nice time?" She stepped a little closer. Her lips were ruinous, ill-treated things stranded in white powder.

My face felt dead and useless, like something frozen. "I'm—I'm waiting for somebody," I blurted out, and was astounded at what I had said.

"Oh!" laughed the woman, lifting her eyebrows with mock surprise. "Who are you waiting for?"

Then she touched my arm.

"I haven't got much money," I muttered.

"How much is that?" A hard note had crept into her voice.

"Only a pound," I lied.

"Come along, then—all right, darling? You want to?"

She was tugging at my arm and smiling. "Coming?"

As we hurried along she began to talk briskly and easily.

"What lovely weather, until this nasty rain spoilt it!" she said. We might have been old friends returning home together. I answered all her remarks with a yes or no, and then fell silent. My mind was a turmoil, I could not think clearly. I kept telling myself I was mad to go with her.

"Have you ever been to France?" she flung at me, without pausing in her speech. She spoke as though she had said the same thing hundreds of times.

"No," I answered, and my voice quivered with nervousness. I felt ashamed of my lack of experience, and angry with this woman for bringing it home to me.

"Have you been in this country long?" I gulped.

She shrugged. "Oh, I should say about ten years. Yes, about that. A long time, isn't it?"

The rain increased, and the woman strode forward, so that I lagged behind. "Come on!" she cried indulgently, "d'you want to get soaked through?"

I stared down at the pavement as I walked, unable to bear the glances of passers-by. The woman looked sideways at my face, curiously, during a long gap of silence.

"Cheer up!" she cried. "Why the frown?"

She took my arm, and we strolled along like lovers; only I walked too stiffly, and was unsure of our direction. I kept blundering into her with my unnatural body.

We turned into a deserted, forlorn back street, with tall buildings reared up on both sides. I was lost now.

Suddenly a thought entered my head. It was a morsel of worldly knowledge, something I must have read in a newspaper, perhaps in a Sunday article 'exposing' vice, and I found myself saying wildly: "Do you work for anybody?"

It was as if a barrier had been flung across the pavement. The woman stopped dead and stared into my face. Her smile had vanished; now she was bristling with anger.

"What d'you mean?" she demanded. She looked at me closely, suspiciously, not indulgent now.

I lost my nerve and began to stammer. "Oh, I—I only wondered. It doesn't matter to me."

"Where on earth did you get that idea from?" Her eyes kept

boring into my face. "Good heavens, there aren't any gangsters round here!"

We came to a green door.

"Here we are." And her voice was professional again, friendly, tinged with amusement.

I stood at her side, feeling terribly foolish.

"What weather!" She was shaking out her umbrella. "Let me just find the key, then we'll soon be in the dry. Here it is."

The door swung open and I followed her in. It was exactly like entering a doctor's surgery; I wanted to get the visit over quickly, and I had the same unpleasant thickening sensation inside me, and I felt cornered.

"Just close the door behind you," she called back mechanically. I noticed for the first time what a deep, husky voice she had.

She led the way up the steep narrow stairs rising from the tiny hallway. They were uncarpeted, and the light was dimmed.

The woman was above me, and I gazed at her long back, her fat, tightly-clothed hips. She had taken off the mackintosh, draping it over her arm, and as she went up it dragged against the beige wallpaper, leaving a damp smear.

My heart pounded. A feverish excitement dulled my senses, like an intoxicant. The woman still climbed wearily above me, putting her feet down like weights. We came to a landing, and I heard a mumble of voices behind a closed door. Then more stairs twisted away to the left. At the next landing the woman paused, waiting for me to reach her. I looked down at my feet as I climbed, but when I drew level I was forced to meet her bold stare.

"Go straight in," she said, pointing to a door that stood slightly ajar. "I shan't be a minute."

And she disappeared through another door. I heard a female voice lift up with excitement, high and shrill. It sounded like a greeting in another language.

I was in a small bedroom, which was windowless. The electric light was already burning, the bulb snug in its pink shade, and everywhere looked smooth and neat, yet barren, like a room in a show-house or an hotel. There was a low, wide bed, covered with a blue silk spread, and a cane chair in one corner, near the dressing-table with its little tangle of jewellery and tall blue candlesticks.

I stood motionless, listening for sounds as I tried to calm my hands. It was like a dream. All the desire seemed to have fled from my limbs. I shivered in the cold air of the room, and struggled to recall walking through the streets, as if it had happened months ago. It was so fantastic, being there. I gazed round in amazement, rubbing my forehead. In a few minutes I would wake up. A sentence I had read that evening began to unwind and repeat itself idiotically: 'Look unto Me and be ye saved'.

The woman came into the room.

"Don't stand there!" she cried in irritation, as soon as she saw me. "Take your things off! And don't look so miserable—what's the matter with you?"

Rather taken aback, I had sat down in the cane chair. Now it creaked as I got up hastily to obey her second instruction.

"Heavens, it's chilly in here!" she exclaimed. Kneeling down by the fireplace she plugged in an electric fire of green tin.

She started to unfasten her skirt, bending her head. Her hair fell over her face like a black cloud. Taking off her skirt, she hung it over the chair, then stood before me in her underskirt.

"A pound," she said flatly, holding out her hand, her lips pressed together so that her mouth was a line. I gave her the money.

"And something for the maid?" She looked me straight in the face with a bleak, business-like expression.

I was in confusion, not expecting this. I fumbled in my pockets and at last produced a two-shilling piece, and when the woman saw it she relaxed at once, smiling encouragement at me. She patted my arm and the coin vanished. "Good boy."

She went over to the bed and sat on the edge of it, smoothing the place beside her with her palm.

"Sit down here," she said, smiling.

Sitting on the bed, I gazed stupidly at her. My hands were trembling. She wore only a vest. I had no desire to touch her, and sensed her dim bewilderment.

"You want to see?"

She lifted her vest and held it up. Her loose belly protruded. She had hardly any breasts. I felt my lips curve of their own accord in a slow, foolish smile as my eyes roamed over her naked body.

"Good?"

She gave me some obscene photographs, scattering them over the bed from an envelope, and I stared blankly at them. They were just unreal, quite meaningless enormities, yet I shuddered, and a slight spasm ran through my shoulders, which she must have seen.

"Don't be afraid, darling. Haven't you got a sweetheart to do this for you?"

"No."

"What a shame."

Her pity goaded me. As if belonging to a blind man, my hands groped and found her big thighs, and she gave a cry of pain: "Your hands are cold!" I drew back, startled, and seemed to wake up, and in the same instant a wave of fear rose up, a submerged horror of disease. It was like something out of the past yawning open, a black, churning hole of dread and fascination.

I shrank away and sat forward on the edge of the bed, and the woman at my side shot upright. For a moment she was too dumbfounded to speak. Then she let out a screech of rage.

"What's the matter?"

I felt suddenly very tired, and longed to escape. I did not bother to speak.

"What's wrong? Can't you answer?" The words came to me venomously, but I no longer cared. "What's the matter with you?"

"I was afraid."

"What of?" She was astounded. "Afraid?" She merely shrugged her shoulders, baffled and disgusted. It was beyond her. She waved her hand jerkily, dismissing me and the whole situation. Already she was half-dressed.

"What d'you want?" she demanded, turning back abruptly. Her professional pride was hurt; she still wanted to earn her money.

"I don't know. Nothing." I felt so tired that I had begun to whisper.

She shouted, "Oh, don't be such a stupid fellow! Why are you so silly? I can't waste any more time, you'll have to go now—somebody else is waiting for this room."

She was almost dressed. I sat guiltily, watching her angry dissatisfaction as it ebbed away. Then I shivered again, and my back was slightly convulsed. My head ached, and I put my hands to my face to rub my forehead. I heard the woman cry out as I did this, in an urgent, almost pleading voice:

"Shh! Shh! Don't do that, darling! Stop that, you mustn't do that!" She sounded so shocked that I lifted my head in surprise to look at her. I believe she had thought I was crying.

I slipped on my jacket and made for the door without speaking. Just then the little maid came in. She held open the door for me, standing there demurely, like a dentist's receptionist.

"Good night, sir," she said cheerfully.

I looked back into the room at the woman fastening a stocking, her head lowered. "Good night, dear," she said, though she had not looked up.

"I'm sorry," I said, in a rush of humility and remorse.

"What for?" she asked, raising her head for a second. "Don't be foolish." She smiled to herself.

I descended the dark stairs, and heard the maid call down in her high voice with its strong accent: "The catch is on the right! Will you close the door after you, please, sir?"

v

Now I was safely free I became brave, and longed to go back and cancel the insult of my behaviour. I hated leaving it behind in the prostitute's memory. It was only one more insult to her sex, but it seemed somehow worse than that of an ordinary client who made use of her.

As I stepped into the street I felt old and wise. A strange knowledge filled me with warmth and softness, that I had not experienced before. I could not have said what it was. It turned my heart and lungs to liquid, without entering my mind.

It was getting quite late. The rain had stopped now. I walked swiftly and blindly, thinking over all that had happened.

When I reached the hostel it looked so squalid and depressing that I decided there and then to start searching for lodgings at a private house, with a family. I had not forgotten that scene in the basement of the large house.

But when I went inside I forgot everything else, for on the small card table near the booking-in desk lay a parcel with my name on it. The writing was unfamiliar. I picked it up gratefully and groped my way upstairs. It felt wonderful to be remembered by someone, though I was baffled by the strange handwriting.

In my dormitory one or two of the beds were already occupied, and the men in them were asleep. They were just dim mounds, hardly visible in the poor light. It was like being in a cemetery, surrounded by unknown graves.

I tiptoed to my bed and tried to examine my package in the gloom. It was cylindrical in shape, a sort of hollow canister. When I shook it gingerly, it rattled. Very carefully I tore off the layers of brown paper. In the next room a low voice was grumbling about a stolen or missing razor.

There was a note inside, which fluttered down on to the blanket. It was almost impossible to decipher in that mournful light, but I made out the signature, and a few words. It was from Jessie Hammond; she must have asked Cecil Luce for my address.

I lifted the mystery package in front of my face, peeling off the last covering of paper. It was a tin of some kind. Then I dragged off the lid, and three pears and an apple fell out, rolling into a hollow on the bed. The skins were broken, and the apple was very badly bruised, almost uneatable, but that did not matter. In my excitement I wanted to write back to her at once. Somehow I should have to wait until next day. I ate one of the pears, then replaced the others in the tin. As I bent over, putting back the lid, I thought of the forgotten water-colour in my suitcase. Before going on to look for lodgings, I would take it to one of the galleries. Then I should have some real news to write in my letter of thanks to Jessie. I felt ridiculously happy, suddenly full of plans, shedding my homesickness and the sense of abandonment I had felt, ever since I had arrived in London. I hugged this new feeling, which made me so warm and comfortable, and looked around.

Yorky was perched on his bed, opposite me, unlacing his boots and singing softly to himself. He had just come in. He stopped singing abruptly and stared down at the floor. "The old bitch! The old bitch!" he whispered to himself. Then he began singing again.

# Seven

### i

The next morning, armed with my masterpiece, I wandered up and down the pavement in Bond Street, where I had noticed some galleries. As I stood near one entrance I tried to screw up just enough courage to push open the door and go in. Once in there, I reasoned nervously, things would take their inevitable course and I should not be allowed to escape. I should have to go through with it. All that was necessary was for me to walk in. Surely they were used to dealing with inexperienced young artists? If I found myself tongue-tied, unable to get out a word, I could always stand there and point, and let my painting speak eloquently for itself. But by this time my palms were sweating, my rigid determination beginning to crumble. They would see at once how provincial I was, with my red hands and clumsy voice. The roll I clutched in one clammy hand grew more and more ridiculous and pathetic. Then I thought of the hundreds of paintings they must have seen, and with what distaste they would suffer new ones, and a wave of panic reared up and defeated me. I peered inside once more, wildly, and caught sight of some impossible twilight figure dawdling there, white-collared and grey-suited, with a bored, supercilious face. What a welcome I would get from him, my grimy raincoat flapping round my knees! In relief I went on to find a snack bar. Did it matter if I never became an artist in that way, I asked myself.

I sat at a quick-service counter in New Oxford Street and ate beans on toast, bolting down the greasy food without pleasure, so that I could walk out and merge with the crowds again. There was a stainless-steel mirror at my elbow, and I examined my face in it with morbid curiosity. How I hated eating in these places, goggled at like a freak in a sideshow. I thought with cynical sadness of those steadfast, defiant words of Llewelyn Powys: 'To pour water from a jug, to break bread, to open a bottle of wine, are lordly offices'.

Later on I bought a newspaper and searched down the Accommodation column. An address in Battersea caught my eye. It sounded homely and inviting. The little paragraph even emphasised that the lodger would live in with the family, and enjoy 'a nice friendly atmosphere'. I set off, hoping I should be able to move in immediately. At the hostel I paid each evening for bed and breakfast, which meant I could leave without giving notice. The extra expense of private lodgings was a drawback, but I brushed the thought aside. When my money dwindled away I would get a job easily enough.

The address led me to a decaying house in a square, looking on to some ground at the centre that had once been a garden, with plants lost in cluttered grass, and iron stumps of old railings along the edges, like dead stalks. The house was named Malvern Villa.

I rang the bell, hearing its dry yelp in the depths of the house. Nobody came, so I banged on the door.

"What is it?" wailed a woman's voice. Then the door opened a fraction, and the woman called through the crack. "Who are you? Oh dear, now then. What d'you want?"

"I saw the advert," I began lamely.

"The what? Oh yes—what a nuisance. Go round the back, dear."

There was a tarred lane at the side of the house, leading to gardens and garages, so I assumed that was where she meant. I was curious to see what Mrs. Parker was like.

A woman's head covered with tight blonde curls was poking out of the opening in the wall.

"Here!" she hissed excitedly. "In here!" I wanted to laugh; it was so secretive, her voice, and I wondered if she was only partly dressed and didn't want to show herself.

When I reached the gateway she had disappeared. Then I saw one of the kitchen curtains trembling, and her arm waving madly at me to come in.

I went into the house, but she had vanished again, and now I could hear the movements upstairs. So I wandered through to the living-room, which looked out to the strip of garden along the side of the kitchen wall. It was a fairly large room, but so cluttered with furniture and heaps of clothes that it looked almost small. There was the usual three-piece suite, large and commonplace, and a shiny table and sideboard littered with papers and magazines. A fawn carpet with a design in red and black that was like a drawing of a machine, with cranks and toothed wheels and rods, covered the floor nearly to the skirting board.

I was gazing round incuriously when Mrs. Parker came in. Her head still bristled with curlers.

"Oh excuse me, won't you," she panted, and flopped into the armchair opposite me. "I had to make myself a bit respectable—you got me out of bed."

She smiled coyly, a look of self-commiseration on her rather pallid face. All her colour had gone now. She was a short, fat woman in her thirties, with bleached hair. Her appearance was as untidy as the room's; in fact, the room reflected her. She really detested housework, she explained, to excuse everything. It was such a bore.

"It's all right for some women, isn't it," she went on rapidly. "Some women love it, they'll get up at six to polish the door knocker—that type of thing. I'm not that sort, never will be, I get bored. I suppose that's because I've always been a professional woman."

"Oh yes," I said, and waited. There was no need to do more than appear expectant, I realised.

"I spent years as manageress of a large florist's, before I got married," she said.

This time I only ventured an "Oh". It was full of exaggerated respect, but even that was unnecessary. As Mrs. Parker spoke her mouth kept curving upwards, as if she didn't really believe her own words, and her little sharp eyes darted all over me.

"It was a terrible worry, such a responsibility. I had to see to all the accounts, everything."

"Did you really?" I said.

"When I think of all those figures, I can't believe I ever did it," she gabbled, and gave a funny blurt of laughter. I started to follow suit, but before my smile could ripen, her ruthless fixed gaze had forced me to lower my head.

Her black skirt was too short, and whenever she moved it rode up over her knees. She tugged at it repeatedly and gave me knowing looks.

"I'm sure you'll like it here," she chattered. "My word, what a big family I shall have!" She slapped her legs jovially, then leaned forward and touched my knee.

"Listen," she whispered. She was grinning and her face had begun to look rather hot again. "Will you be *happy* here? That's the important thing, isn't it? Tell me the truth, now."

She glared straight into my face, grinning, in what she thought was a frank gaze. But it was half desperate, humourless, almost plaintive, and I turned red with embarrassment.

"Yes, I think so," I murmured politely.

"So do I!" She was strangely triumphant. "As soon as I saw you sitting there, I said to myself, 'He'll be happy with us!' What d'you think of that? Isn't that amazing?"

"Yes," I laughed, still not understanding her. When I got to know her better I heard double meanings in almost everything she said to me. You had to tread with care, as if you were walking down an icy street and looking perfectly safe to the eye.

"Come along, then," she beamed, "and I'll show you where you're going to sleep. You may as well see it now."

"I've got to fetch my suitcase from the hostel yet," I protested weakly, but she grabbed my hand and led me through the hall to the stairs. She dropped her playfulness and became business-like as she stood in the small bedroom with her hands on her hips, surveying everything. We struggled with a Sheraton wardrobe, trying to drag it back into a corner, while she chattered and panted, telling me about another new lodger she was expecting.

"He's a waiter at a big hotel. He came to see me a week ago today. Isn't that strange! Oh, he's a lovely boy, full of pranks."

We stood away from the wardrobe, sighing.

"Oh!" Mrs. Parker gasped, "I'm out of breath!" Stepping back against a bed she pretended to fall, clutching my arm so that I was almost jerked off my feet. As we floundered about she pawed at me half seriously, breathing hard and giggling.

I soon discovered that she had no tactics, no preliminaries. And the same treatment was meted out to all newcomers. She tried her luck with everybody, relying on a combination of coyness and sheer brawn. It was the coyness which made me wince, because I sensed something harsh and unfeeling underneath. "I love a bit of fun," she would say, but I knew she was not playing at all. Her attempts at seduction would have been pitiful if she had not been such a dynamo of crude energy, her hair-pins dropping out and her face red and shiny, like a flabby tomato.

She was persistent as a bird, so it was impossible to ignore her. Her husband was a tall, dark-faced man with prominent dog-like eyes; from Exeter. She had met him during a holiday one summer at Southsea. He came dashing in at six with his haversack and rough blue canvas raincoat, and made a formal demand for his meal. It happened nearly every evening, and always with the same result.

"Come on, Gladys—move," he said. "You've 'ad time. What have you been at all day?"

Already he was stripping off his jacket and rolling back his sleeves, ready to get down on his knees with a brush and dustpan. I used to try to decide whether he did this as a kind of silent criticism of the state of everything, or out of some wild belief that he would eventually convert his wife to cleanliness by his example.

Sometimes she made excuses, putting a little whine in her voice; but if she felt irritable, she threatened: "How dare you yell at me in front of guests? I do my best, I can't do more, can I? Now shut up."

"You're bloody hopeless, you are," he would mutter, on his hands and knees, working. Finally he got up without a word and went to the table for his dinner, attacking the food in silence. You could tell by his back how angry he was. Gladys would often make a lunge at him, rubbing her hand over his head before he had time to jerk away. It was strange to see him looking suddenly tousled, when he was always so neat, his black crinkly hair perfectly parted. I disliked him on sight, but when his wife and the two sons exchanged derisive glances behind his back, I felt sorry for him.

ii

I had been at Malvern Villa for three weeks. One Tuesday morning Gladys surprised me by bringing a cup of tea into my bedroom. This was so abnormal that I wondered what was to follow. She sat on my bed as I sipped at the tea, making a few complaints about Fred, her husband, which I had heard before. Then she asked me to guess what he had said about me last night, when they were lying in bed together.

"What did he say?" I asked suspiciously.

"He said that you're close." There was a pleased, vindictive look on her face, as though she thoroughly approved.

For a moment I could not think what she meant. Then I laughed. So that was what Fred thought of me!

"Perhaps he's right," I said.

"You're not close, you're just quiet," she answered, and smirked at me, as if to say, "I understand everything."

I still did not have a job. I kept putting it off. So I would sometimes wake up to find the house silent. And nearly every morning, after I got up, there would be a tussle. I had to devise tactics of my own to ward Gladys off. It was all 'in fun', but I knew now what desperation lay behind those words. I would stand there as calm as a policeman, gazing deeply and amusedly into her face. I was amazed at my own boldness. I never knew what made me hit upon this absurd lion-tamer's trick, but it nearly always worked, and I came to regard it as my best defence. It made her uneasy about her self-respect. "Oh you!" she would gasp in embarrassment, and push me off playfully. At least, it was meant to be playful. It sent me staggering back across the room. I felt like an actor in a silent comedy film, and often wished for Charlie Chaplin's agility. Her bosom heaved violently during these strenuous bouts, as she wheezed and fought for breath, blurting out the same things each time. "I wonder if you *like* me? Sometimes I think you do—but I wouldn't dream of asking you. It wouldn't be right!" I made my eyes as eloquent as possible because I never knew what to say.

Once or twice real pity crept into them. Now and then I

felt my iron control weakening, and a fatal warmth, a sympathy, slipped in. It was impossible to keep up a poker face for ever.

She had bursts of energy, when her short body charged about the house, her face brick-red as she made some attempt to clear up the mess. This lasted perhaps half an hour, until she languished again, overwhelmed by boredom and wretchedness. When I entered the kitchen she usually affected a demure air for a few moments; then she would abandon all pretence and flop down in a chair to talk. The conversation ran on vaguely, but always swerved back to the unanswerable problem of herself. Did I think she was fit for nothing better than this? Would I understand if she told me something of her past? Did I imagine she was an average woman?

Because I was new, and listened to her, I was her favourite of the moment. She came into me once as I sat up in bed in my pyjamas, and told me I needed fattening up. If I kept it a secret, she would give me more eggs than the others.

"You're too thin," she said. She sat at the bottom of the bed, fat and slovenly, sagging inside her mauve dressing-gown.

"Yes, I know," I admitted ruefully. I was rather ashamed of my body because I thought it ugly. All my ribs showed and my shoulder-blades stuck out. I felt as thin as a wire.

"Have you got T.B.?" she asked hopefully. She thought there was something romantic and poetic about the disease. She often said she would like to care for someone who was utterly helpless. Then she would know that she was needed. I flinched at the thought of being nursed by her.

After a while I came to accept her. She would never be any different, and the household would have been morbid and lifeless without her.

But I could never reconcile myself to her husband. Fred was a reader of electricity meters. I think I despised him so much because he was such a denizen of the city, like a sewer rat, scurrying in and out of the tubes. In the evening he sat for hours with his newspaper, completely engrossed. It was a sickening ritual. If someone interrupted him during this period, his stricken, outraged face appeared slowly over the top of the paper, as if a horrible mistake had been made. Then his head sank down again, like a sour moon dropping out of sight.

Gladys eyed him at all times with pitiless, withering contempt. The only thing she ever said in his favour was that he was a hard worker. But she jeered at him mercilessly before the others, carrying on a private quarrel under the camouflage of a trivial argument.

"Stop it, Auntie, for God's sake!" cried her niece once, and went slamming out of the house in disgust.

Now and then Fred turned and rebelled, drawing back his lips as he let loose a tyrannical little outburst, his fists clenched. But after one of her cruel braying laughs he always slunk back into his corner with the paper, beaten.

### iii

Four of us slept in the bedroom I occupied. The two sons had camp beds, one on each side of the window. As I was the last to be fitted in, I had to share the only double bed with a young ex-soldier, the other lodger. I was asked very nicely if I objected, but in any case there was no alternative. It was either that or nothing. But because of this inconvenience I was allowed a cheaper rate.

On my first visit I had been told by Gladys what wonderful boys these two sons of hers were. How fortunate it was to have such lively, entertaining companions, she said. They were so intelligent, so gay and amusing—David especially. He made her ache with laughter. Apparently Edmund was the more studious of the two, but he was a charming, kindly fellow, witty and cultured. She went on and on, painting a glowing picture for me. They were twins, about to leave school.

After a week of their company I had had enough of them. Their idiotic jokes and horseplay only depressed me; it seemed more like hysteria than high spirits. I wondered when they settled down and studied for the difficult examination they kept mentioning. And after seeing them sauntering off to school, then rushing back half way through the afternoon to begin another gay shindy, I decided to make my period of unemployment last as long as possible. At least they had countered some of the effects of Fred and his will-to-work. Fred had become the embodiment of my conscience.

Edmund was an enthusiastic member of the Boys' Brigade. With his owlish, mildly astonished gaze behind large shell spectacles, he reminded me of one whenever I saw him. He did not need to be in uniform. Looking at him I could not help remembering a week I had spent once at a scout camp, when I was eleven. We dug latrines and cleaned out greasy tins while one of the seniors lounged and joked, watching over us benevolently. I was not keen on youth movements.

David was more of a roughneck, short and squat like his brother, yet somehow very different in his behaviour and his expressions. His mother adored him, and could see nothing but irresistible energy and brilliance shining forth. Oh, he was going to do wonderful things—who could possibly resist him? In return he cheeked her shamelessly, and when she turned her back his eyes rolled up in sophisticated amusement. He threw himself around in the house like a savage, as if there was a devil inside him; and Edmund copied him. Watching them both, you guessed that without David to whip him into a frenzy, Edmund would have been a reasonably quiet and normal boy. But they were hardly ever apart, so it remained a theory.

In an awkward, gawky, off-hand sort of way, both of them were after Carol, their fifteen-year-old cousin who lived with them, though her manners were atrocious, and she seemed to give them no encouragement. I hardly ever heard her speak a friendly word to them, or to anyone. She would have tantrums with clockwork regularity, then sulk in a chair for hours afterwards. "Don't take any notice," her aunt used to say, winking across at one of us. "It's because she's at a difficult age." The sliding, insidious attack in this kind of remark very often caught Carol on the raw, and she would jerk up just like her uncle and fling out an insult about her aunt's age or figure. These outbursts had a deadly female sting to them, a knowledge of where to strike. Then it was the other's turn to let out a little gasp of pain and begin to weep, while her lachrymose nagging wailed out between the sobs. She was not as tough as her niece.

One evening I sat in the living-room, trying to write to Jessie.

After receiving the parcel I had written back to her, and since then our letters had been going back and forth. She told me how sick she was of Birmingham, how mean and small a world it was. She longed to get away, as I had done. She did not know what she wanted to do; her desires were all negative. She admired me for uprooting myself, she said, and reading her words I glowed with pride, though I felt far from admirable. London was no better than Birmingham, I informed her pompously, forgetting that she had been across the Atlantic and back. She would not agree, her determined words speeding back to me by return post. I enjoyed our delayed-action battles, and I refused to give way. London was only bigger, and sprawled more, I declared. It was just a bigger ugliness. And she insisted that it was cosmopolitan and free, different in spirit altogether. Only a few weeks ago I should have agreed with her.

I sat at the living-room table, crouched over my writing-pad, while Gladys leaned back in an armchair and watched me, pretending to darn a sock. She poked away at it indifferently, her legs crossed. I waited for her mischief to start; I had got to know her thoroughly now. When she was faced with any housework she cast around for distractions.

"I think he's handsome, don't you?" she called suddenly to her niece, and as she spoke she leered coyly at me.

I was used to this kind of comment, thrown out to stir up a little activity. But I was not ready for what followed.

"What—him?" screeched Carol. She loaded her voice with sarcasm, jerking upright in her chair, her magazine forgotten. "He's nothing but a stuck-up prig. You never know what he's thinking, he never lets on! Why doesn't he join in the fun sometimes, like Edmund and Dave? If he thinks he's too good for us, too high-and-mighty, what does he stay here for?"

Her sharp little face, usually so stony and expressionless, was flushed with her passion. I sat perfectly still, saying nothing. I felt numbed by her words. It was probably quite true, her accusation, but why did she make so much of it? Why did it insult her personally? I began to smoulder with anger, then harden slowly into hatred.

"Don't be so silly," her aunt was protesting feebly. "You mustn't say such things to our guest. Your manners lately, my girl—really, I don't know. Just because Nick's a quiet boy, and prefers his own company . . ." and she turned to me, smiling her soft smile of satisfaction. She had created an emotional disturbance. "He's quite entitled to be like that, as far as I'm concerned. I think he's a nice boy."

But the secret was out. I felt it expressed an unspoken grudge which they all shared. After that the atmosphere of the house seemed oppressive, and I kept away from it as long as possible. And I had noticed how surreptitiously the twins disappeared, quietly slipping out when they had swallowed their evening meal. Perhaps they had had their fill of such scenes. So I followed suit. It was better to be in the streets, even with nowhere to go, than sit watching Fred absorbing newsprint in that room.

I looked forward to seeing Arthur, my sleeping partner, when I came in to go to bed. I knew he worked at some local government offices, but for a long time I did not know what he did there. It was difficult to get anything out of him. I felt a kinship between us because he came from the Midlands. The others merely nodded to him or ignored him. He had hardly any conversation, and no talk whatever, and Fred regarded him as he would have an imbecile.

We used to lie side by side in the dark room and have brief conversations, before David and Edmund came bursting in from a cinema, or their street corner college. Arthur made a habit of smoking a cigarette in bed before settling down to go to sleep, and I was reminded of Yorky at the hostel. It was strange to hear him beside me, breathing deeply and puffing out, as if he had endless time. Although I did not smoke I found comfort and relaxation in listening to his sounds and gazing at his glowing cigarette-end.

He lay very straight, keeping carefully to his half of the bed. I wondered if the thought of our bodies touching by accident filled him with distaste; for that was how it affected me at first, sleeping with a stranger, until I forgot about it.

Downstairs he sat about in a lost way, waiting for a meal, or killing time, before going off to the cinema or a pub. He always sat motionless with his hands drooping between his knees, a cigarette burning away in his fingers. His face was impassive, and he looked up at everybody with his pale, moony eyes, like an uncomprehending animal, and dropped ash on the carpet.

He was dully inarticulate, and seemed to silence himself after a few words, so our conversations at night did not lead anywhere, or amount to much. After one or two exchanges we fell silent. But it suited me, after listening to the mental fireworks and general knowledge debates of the twins. I was in no mood for that. Our talks made no demands; we spoke if we felt like it, and stopped when we didn't want to bother.

I learned gradually that he had suffered some kind of accident in the army, and worked now as a cleaner. He cleaned a few offices before nine in the morning, then waited near the switchboard as a relief telephone operator for the rest of the day. That was all he had to do. I asked if the time dragged badly, with so little to occupy him.

"It does that," he said.

I waited for him to go on, but he had finished.

One night he told me that he came from Bickleigh, a mining village near Nuneaton. I said that Bedworth was the only small place that side of Coventry I had heard of.

"Oh ay," he said, "I know Bed'orth. It's about two mile from Bickleigh."

I pricked up my ears at once, and asked him if he had ever heard of George Eliot, the writer, who was born at Bedworth.

There was no answer. He kept drawing in air and smoke, slowly and steadily, in and out, lying motionless in the bed beside me. The moon had risen, beginning to light the room. Before the open window the curtains fluttered, lifting and sinking back. I stared at them and waited. Arthur was thinking. I knew better than to repeat the question.

"Ay," he said at last. "Ay, I've 'eard summat."

And that was all I could get out of him. But this time I was not satisfied; I wanted him to go on talking, and tried something different, asking him now what he thought of living in a city. What did he think of London, and how did it compare with country life? It was a stupid question. Hanging there, in the dense silence, it even *sounded* foolish.

I hardly expected him to answer. Then he cleared his throat.

"I don't think owt about it," he said slowly, in a loud gloomy voice. "Where I cum from, people are friendly to yer, like."

I warmed towards him, and suddenly his village became a wonderful place, though it was probably hideous with mean cottage-hovels and slag heaps, sunk in the midst of the industrial country. But he had made it sound human and desirable, a warm, living place. I felt like grabbing his hand under the sheets to congratulate him.

He would say no more. Apart from the usual grunts of assent he was finished. Nothing could make him speak now. I felt mildly angry with him for a moment, because he seemed so imperturbable, like a tortoise. He was back inside his shell, refusing to poke out his head, and I was banging away on the glazed surface, all to no purpose. He was far underneath. I envied him for being so indifferent and self-sufficient.

The only person who ever managed to rouse him to eloquence was Gladys. Apparently he had been left alone in the house with her, and she had been up to her pranks, for one night as we lay silent in the dark room, he suddenly blurted out: "That bloody woman down there makes me feel proper daft! Ignorant, that's what she is!"

iv

Jessie's letters came as regularly as ever, and I was grateful for them. They helped to keep up my spirits. But I tried not to think of how helpless I would be now if they stopped. My eagerness for them did not escape Gladys; she struggled for a time to contain her curiosity, but one day she had to ask what they were.

"Is that your sweetheart who writes to you all the time?" she asked, tilting her nose. She was offended because I had not offered any information.

I laughed. "No, not exactly," I said.

"Go on," she said. "She must be, writing as often as that."

"I've only met her once," I said. Already I was telling her more than I intended.

"Bet you've got a photo," she said cunningly.

I shook my head, grinning, and began to enjoy the mystery I had created.

"You haven't?" She examined my face. "I don't believe you. I think you're a dark horse," she said, with an amiable intonation that I distrusted.

"It's true."

She decided to be hurt. "All right," she said, in a queer gulpy voice, and flounced into the kitchen.

When Jessie mentioned in her next letter that she was thinking of coming to London the following Saturday, I could hardly believe it. Would I care to meet the train at Euston, she asked. It was too good to be true. I wrote back immediately, a naïve, enthusiastic letter, then tried to put it all out of my mind, so that the days would pass quickly. But I kept circling back in my thoughts to this approaching visit. I asked myself why I was so absurdly happy, and fought against it, for it seemed mad and dangerous. If something happened and it fell through, the disappointment would be ghastly, I reasoned. But wherever I went I was whispering and tingling in my veins with a secret excitement, so that in the end I longed for it without restraint. And on Saturday morning my happiness rose up so powerfully that everything else was swept aside.

The train she would come on started from Liverpool. It was late. Gradually, as I paced up and down, I got into a state of tension, my courage and eagerness seeping away. I thought of the ordeal of meeting her, after all the wild nonsense I had written.

Then, as I looked once more at the Arrivals board, the hissing train ran in and halted, and passengers began to step down. With a little shock of surprise I saw Cecil Luce. I did not know he was coming. Jessie jumped down beside him and saw me almost at once, her arm lifting to wave excitedly. It was a jerky, childish greeting. I signalled back, not knowing whether to walk forward or wait. It was good to see Cecil again, his hair specially oiled and snug. He had not seen me. He slouched along at her side, still in his brown suit, turning his head slowly and blindly, as though confused by so much activity. Jessie held his arm in a firm grip. She seemed to be steering him through the crowds towards me.

Still he did not give any sign of recognition until they were only a few yards away. Jessie was laughing and pointing.

"There!" she cried. "See him now?"

I believe he had forgotten what I looked like.

"How's life, old man?" he said. His head lolled to one side a little, his large mouth slightly open, wet and coarse-looking. He shambled up and took my hand and crushed it, glaring benevolently into my face.

As we walked to the barrier Jessie explained that Cecil was on his way to visit his married sister, who kept a café in Deptford. Her words hardly made sense. I was dazzled by her. She was very beautiful in green velvet, though taller and darker than I had remembered. Also there was something strained and perplexed on her forehead that I had not noticed before. She did not veil her eyes, but looked frankly and inquisitively at me, and my heart leapt in my chest.

Out in the bustling street I turned to Cecil.

"Whereabouts is Deptford?" I asked.

Jessie tipped up her chin and laughed, hugging my arm a moment. It seemed perfectly natural.

"What a Londoner you are, asking us!" she cried.

"I know, but I only know the centre," I said, smiling. "It's such a vast place."

"D'you know Greenwich at all?" said Cecil. "Where the Observatory is?"

"Yes, I've been there, once."

"Well, that's Deptford, near enough."

Finally we decided to go with Cecil to Greenwich, then he would leave us and go to his sister's. He was staying there for the week-end, but Jessie was returning the same day on a late train. I wanted to shake Cecil off, yet at the same time I wanted to be friendly. So I was happy with this arrangement. And for the time being I felt too awkward and nervous to be left alone with Jessie. I was glad of Cecil's company.

We travelled through the city, through a web of foggy streets, swerving and twisting, rumbling down hills, snoring up them, until I was dizzy. I was completely lost. We sat on the top of the bus, swaying, and I began to feel shaken and sick. I had hung back

so that Jessie and Cecil were forced to sit together, slipping into
the seat behind them. It gave me a slight advantage, for I was
able to look at her without being observed. Now and then she
twisted her head to speak. I knew I was being perverse, that I
really longed to be alone with her, but I was afraid of spoiling
everything before I properly composed myself.

As we flashed by a dance hall, down the last incline, I thought
I sensed an apprehension in her, a fear of being left with me,
though perhaps I was mistaken. I groaned inwardly at my timidity, and kept telling myself that if she had not wanted to see me
she would never have come.

Later on we were climbing Observatory hill. Cecil had gone,
and I was amazed that things were happening so simply and naturally. I had not really needed him at all. It was a meek day in early
November, and now a watery sun broke through, hanging over
us, very mild and indirect.

"That's an English sun," said Jessie, as we tramped forward
over the shabby grass.

"How d'you mean?" I asked breathlessly.

"No passion in it," she laughed, and gave me a mock-wicked
look. As she marched along she kicked at heaps of leaves and scattered them.

"I like doing that," she chuckled. "Aren't I destructive?"

She lashed out with her foot again at a mound of leaves.
"Whoosh!" she shouted, and burst out laughing. I felt she was
deliberately trying to ease the tension between us, and a rush
of gladness went through me, to think that she understood. I
was conscious too of the lovely tenderness of an older woman
towards someone of my age, someone younger than herself. It
was nothing like a girl's sweetness: different altogether, and much
deeper, with a subtle, rather wistful flattery in it. How she loved
having me in charge, sometimes; yet in another part of her she
was childish, quick, with exuberant gestures. I watched her and
brimmed with admiration, enjoying all her movements. I longed
for the darkness to come, so that I could kiss her.

We wandered near the Observatory, looking out over the city,
across to Hampstead, walking along without speaking.

"Say something!" she demanded, and pouted her lips, pretending to be angry. "Aren't you glad I've come?"

I recognised the challenge, though she was gently playful. She looked at me wide-eyed and waited, her mouth tinged with mischief.

"Yes, I'm glad," I said softly. I felt that words did not matter. They were a clumsiness.

She was silent for a time.

"Did you mean those things, in your letters?" came her low voice. I was afraid to look at her then, and could only nod without answering, seeing her eyes shine with quick tenderness.

Afterwards I found my tongue. I pointed out St. Paul's, hovering low over Tower Bridge, half-lost in smoke. We started back down the hill towards the river. It was better there than at Westminster, I told her, because the river had a sea-smell.

"Cecil's a dear, you know," she said suddenly.

"Are you sorry we left him?" I asked.

"Silly boy, I'm awfully fond of him, but I'm glad we got rid of him!" And she laughed. "Aren't you?"

"Need you ask?" I said.

We found a café overlooking the river, and sat there over our coffee for a while. I had never been so quietly happy. Outside it was low water; there was even a narrow ribbon of beach.

"How lovely it is now," she cried. "Like an early Gauguin." She was peering through the small cracked window at her elbow, looking out at the concrete pier, and some thick iron sticking out of the sunken water. It would have been a forlorn scene, but the light was touching it magically.

"I don't care for him," I said quickly, determined to air my knowledge. "I prefer Van Gogh." Which was true.

"Oh yes, but Gauguin's design is much better," she protested.

"Maybe it is," I said. "I didn't mean that. I just don't like him as a man, that's all. He was just a bored banker looking for thrills. Van Gogh strikes me as genuine—even though he's so deadly serious about everything. I doubt if he ever laughed out loud, poor Van Gogh."

I stopped, confused by my sudden speech. Jessie was listening to every word, alert and intense. I felt I had talked too cleverly, and drew back inside myself a little.

"Is that why you like him—because he never laughed?" Jessie asked, smiling. "How queer you are."

"I suppose I am," I admitted. "Perhaps that's why he attracts me. We'd have made a good pair."

"How d'you mean?" she laughed. "Will you go mad and lop off your ear, as well?"

"No, not exactly," I said. "I don't mind ears. Tongues are our biggest curse, I think. We'd be saner without tongues—and much happier, too."

She made herself shudder. "Horrible! Imagine us sitting here now and clucking at each other!"

We both laughed. Then she was suddenly serious.

"Do you still write your poems?" she asked, her eyes resting gently on my face.

"Now and then."

"What a pity you don't write a lot of them."

"Perhaps I will, one day, but I'm not in the mood for them just now. The world's too realistic, too harsh a place, at the moment. I feel if I try to be lyrical I shall end up like Gauguin, with those painted-tin skies of his, propped up with hills cut out of cardboard, and lamp-post trees."

She gasped with laughter, a little shocked. "You devil!" she exclaimed. "You really do dislike him, don't you? Why?"

"He was a fake, and he started off all this abstraction stuff. I know it was bound to come without him, but its nice to blame somebody. He was the father of it, you know. Not Cézanne. Old Cézanne was right to despise him."

"I still say he had a wonderful sense of design," she countered stubbornly.

We argued on happily, then I suggested we could get another bus and pay a visit to the Tate.

"Wonderful!" she cried, jumping to her feet.

"Shall we get a meal somewhere first?" I asked her, when we were nearly at Millbank.

"No, I'm too excited to eat much. How about you?" And she turned to examine me anxiously.

I grinned. "Oh I can go for hours—days, sometimes," I exaggerated.

V

Then it was evening, and I felt cheated by the time which had slipped away so quickly. We ran into a tube entrance, glad to escape the Saturday night traffic, the surging crowds near Trafalgar Square. In a few minutes we were at the clanging dark station.

When we reached the right platform, Jessie discovered that she had mistaken the departure time. Her train was not due out for another hour and three-quarters. So we went out again and wandered through the dismal streets around Euston, which were empty and dark. Occasional windows bled yellow light on the pavement. There were one or two sordid-looking men loitering at corners or standing back sinister in the shadows. As we crossed the bare asphalt a dreariness took hold of me.

In front of us a man halted abruptly. He fingered the white scarf wound tightly around his neck, and spat a gob of yellow phlegm into the gutter near a drain. Then he held his nose between thumb and finger and cleared both his nostrils.

"My God," I heard Jessie say. She had turned her head aside in disgust.

She edged closer and took my arm, as if afraid.

"I hate louts," she said bitterly, in a low voice.

"I know," I said.

She seemed to be clinging to me as we walked, and I imagined I was guiding and protecting her, though I knew it was not true.

"I was thinking," she said, "as he did that, of how rare you are, with your Van Gogh and your poems." She spoke almost in defiance, as if she expected someone to attack her words. All I could think of was the soft pressure of her hand on my arm. I kept trying to steel myself to kiss her.

"It's no joke, being different," I said grimly.

"Don't change, though. Or I shan't like you."

"No fear of that," I laughed.

Somehow, without my mentioning it, she grew curious about Malvern Villa. To her it was just an address on an envelope. She asked if I had a good landlady.

"I wouldn't say she was morally good. She's always looking for a lover."

"Oh lord," she cried, horrified. "Does she pester *you*?"

"Quite often," I boasted calmly. "I'm her favourite, at the moment. Everybody else keeps out of her way, that's why."

"Can't you do that? Why on earth do you stay there? I should hate it, I really should." She was concerned, but her concern was swiftly becoming anger. "Why do you put up with it, Nick?" she persisted, in an incredulous voice.

"I don't know," I confessed. "Perhaps for the company—no, it's not just that. I just haven't bothered about moving, I don't know why."

"How do you paint in such a place, or do anything you want?"

"I can't."

"Then why not find a little room of your own? Why don't you, Nick? It would be fun—and there must be plenty to let."

"All right—I will," I said.

"Don't you want to?"

"I've often thought about it."

We decided to go no farther away from the station, and went back slowly. A small battered car limped past us and we both watched it come to a standstill at the next corner, trembling in front of a chemist's shop. Nobody got out.

As we entered a patch of thick darkness, where a street light was damaged, I looked at the white blotch of her face, gathering my courage.

"I wish we had somewhere to go," I said.

She laughed low in her throat.

Somehow we had stopped on the pavement. She took my hand in silence, taking charge again, and drew me in to the wall.

"Find a room for us, then," she whispered huskily. "Will you?"

She put up her face very simply, closing her eyes. I took her in my arms quickly, before someone came. I would have hated it if anyone had seen us. But no one was about.

"Will you?" came her muffled voice, wistfully.

In less than an hour she had gone, and I was plunging back in the opposite direction, along the platform.

# *Eight*

She had promised to come again the following Saturday. I went about waiting for this day, going over all our conversations and thinking of more intelligent things I could have said, and more important things I had left unsaid, which I would say next time. My sense of futility and emptiness was gone now. And I kept smiling to myself as I thought of her suggestions, when she said: "Why don't you join a life class? Why not get a room, so that you can paint? Have you ever done any modelling? Would you like me to show you—I'm sure you'd be good at it." What was all that to me now? Perhaps later I would turn to it again, but I could not imagine it. An old, deeply submerged longing rose up, to love a woman, to be married and to know common joys. Until that happened I was only waiting, marking time, wasting my life. I wanted to be married. Everything else could wait. I meant to find out as soon as possible if Jessie was the one; if not, I must get involved with someone else. I longed violently for something to happen, wanting to speed things up, feeling helpless and impotent because I could not.

A small shop not far from Malvern Villa had been taken over by a palmist. I went past it regularly, and noticed one day that the 'To Let' signs had disappeared. Then on the Monday after Jessie's visit the window was filled with cardboard diagrams of huge hands, yellowish and frowsty, covered in fine black lines. There were six gruesome enlarged photographs of hands belonging to different people; actors, celebrities, criminals, with black arrows pointing confidently to various characteristics.

Going past on Tuesday I slowed down, and something made me stop outside the window. What would the palmist make of my hand, I wondered. I felt certain that things were moving towards some sort of climax. My money was getting low, but I stood there picturing my future circumstances being revealed, my new, unknown self leaping out at me, and the temptation was too great. I pushed open the door and went in hastily, before I was able to change my mind.

I was in a tiny waiting-room, with two cheap chairs which had been enamelled a blood red, and in an alcove was a short counter. No one seemed to be about. A bell clattered weakly somewhere inside the house, worked by the door, and I looked towards a mysterious opening which had a magenta curtain hung in front of it, flapping slightly in the draught I had made.

Suddenly this curtain moved aside, and a stout jovial woman beamed up at me.

"Come in, will you!" she said emphatically, giving the words a brisk professional emphasis. "Be careful—there are three little steps here."

She stood waiting, holding the curtain back, as I stepped down gingerly to the lower floor level.

"There we are!" she said in triumph, and let the curtain fall behind her.

This place was even smaller than the ante-room, and just as bare. On one wall hung a dark oil painting of Christ, his eyes rolling back in his head ecstatically. The room was poorly lighted and dusty. In one corner was a tiny round table with a shiny surface the colour of strong tea, and two more crimson chairs.

"You like my Jesus?" asked the woman quickly. "He was a present—the artist gave him to me. Sit down, will you?"

She seated herself opposite me, and sat like an oracle, to impress me. But there was an energy about her which destroyed the effect. I liked her at once. She was dressed in black, quite plain, yet there was an odd, foreign touch. Her pouched eyes, black and quick, were humorous in her puffy face. All her movements were deft, surprising me, though this is not uncommon with heavy people.

"I am German," she said immediately, without ceremony, "so you must sometimes excuse my speech—you understand?" She laid her neat white hand on her plump bosom.

"Yes, I see," I said faintly.

"Now then—can I haf your hand?"

I held it out stiffly. She took it with great care in her two small hands, cradling it, as though it were a work of art. I glowed with pleasure. It seemed a subtle compliment.

She began to talk continuously about the lines of my hand, speaking in a rather involved way, perhaps to impress me, and I did not pay much attention to it. It was a pseudo-scientific language. But I liked her warm juicy voice, and was fascinated by the queer stress she put on certain words, and her bubbling Continental vitality. There was something open and charming about her.

"You haf good fingers," she said briskly. "Good. Good shape. You know this? And this curve down to the thumb—here—you see? That iss good also. Quite different to mine—see that? Very bad. You are lucky not to be like me!"

"I didn't know there was so much to see," I said, wanting to flatter her. The woman's bright eyes sparkled with appreciation, then she bent her head again to scrutinise my palms. She asked for the left hand, and I lifted it and put it forward. Then she wanted the right again, and I saw her frown, as if puzzled.

"You are married, yes?" she said quickly, looking into my face. "How many children haf you?"

I laughed, telling her that I was single.

"What iss that—eh? What?" She could hardly believe it. There seemed real astonishment in her voice.

"But it iss all here—look here, this line—look!" she cried. "Do you mean it?"

She asked again for my age.

"Twenty-five this month," I told her.

"Incredible!" She scrutinised my hands again, darting from one to the other. "Many years ago you should have been married. Four, five years. Yes. Yes." She nodded vigorously. "And children, too—you should haf children. How plain it iss—no mistake at all. Yet you say none? Oh, it could happen any time, any time now! It is long delayed, oh yes."

She looked up, warm with excitement, nodding sagely.

"I hope so," I said, smiling. "It makes sense, anyway."

"Of course—quite sure!" she cried. Then from the peak of this discovery, buoyed up by her excitement, she looked once more at my hands to divine the future.

"You are different, not like another man—different to him," she pronounced. "You will do something special, not with a machine. Maybe invent, maybe artistic—different. So." And she leaned back and beamed across at me, releasing my hands. I thought she had finished, but as I began to rise she touched my arm. "Listen. You will do something else. Understand? And you must do it mit your own brain, and tell nopody!"

I thanked her, and was surprised because she only asked for half a crown. I would have given her much more. It was wonderful to be confirmed in your desires. She bustled me to the door, and I left her, full of respect for palmistry. Afterwards I thought of how shrewd and clever she must have been, to look at my hands and at the same time read the story in my face.

ii

I was still searching for a room of my own, reading advertisements and going off to unknown districts. They were all too expensive. Eventually I went back to Greenwich. The place had a kind of glamour for me now, and I thought I should like to live there. Someone directed me to a large, tall house that had been converted into apartments. The owner lived out of London, I was told, but a tenant on the ground floor was also the janitor; he and his wife looked after the whole building and collected rents.

He was a stout, gloomy man with ringed eyes and a long head. When I said I would take the vacant room he told me he wanted to clean it out first, and distemper the walls.

"The last tenant was filthy," he said in his melancholy voice. "So I got him out, the dirty bugger."

He took me downstairs to meet his wife. Mrs. Lawton was Welsh. She had a round, white, flaccid face. Her over-fat arms were a greyish colour, like the underside of a slug, and her large eyes, glassy and pathetic, always seemed on the verge of tears. In a monotonous singsong voice she ended almost every sentence with 'you know', as if tying a weight to it. As she started to speak I was reminded of Gladys, but a Gladys who had lost all hope. Her voice, genteel and snobbish, full of complaint, seemed pitifully gutted of vitality. It told a tale of dirty slops, bleak rooms and curtains soiled with soot. It was respectability on its last legs.

When I gave Gladys a week's notice I expected her to make a scene. But she was not even surprised.

"I thought you'd be off," she said calmly. "Don't forget to look us up sometime, when you're down this way."

I was relieved. After a few days I went back to Greenwich, walking about in the unfamiliar streets where I did not belong. I hated Battersea now. On Friday I went with my suitcase, and Mr. Lawton took me up to inspect his distempering. My room was on the first landing, the door directly opposite a rusty gas stove which I would share with another tenant.

Mr. Lawton gazed round fondly, delighted with his handi-work. "Rose pink and daffodil," he croaked at me in confidence. "Sort of fresh, spring-like. Wonderful what a bit of colour-wash will do."

I was looking round in dismay. The woodwork was pink. To me it seemed as hideous and oppressive as Van Gogh's *Night Café*. My heart sank when I thought of bringing Jessie. Later I discov-ered that every room in the house had been distempered this awful pink colour; no doubt there were gallons of it in the cellar.

I stood there, still holding my suitcase. This was my first expe-rience of bed-sitting-rooms, and the paunchy janitor seemed to sense my bewilderment.

"Don't be afraid to ask if you want anything," he said drearily. "The wife's always around, if you go down to the kitchen. She'll show you where the meters are, for the gas. Watch your coppers or you'll have one jam in the slot, like the bloke upstairs did yes-terday."

He had retreated until his body was out of sight behind the door. All I could see was his mournful face, wobbling and grin-ning at me. Suddenly he lifted his head and stared up at the elec-tric bulb in the centre of the ceiling. "And whatever you do," he yelled, "don't leave the light on in the passage!"

I waited for him to descend the stairs before closing the door, listening to the filtered noises from above and below. Then I examined my bed under the window. It had coarse dark blankets and dingy sheets. Through the window I could see down into a timber yard. There were rusty corrugated-iron sheds and high orderly stacks of pale yellow wood. I decided, as I looked, to go out next day and buy a linen sleeping-bag for the bed. The sheets filled me with distaste, and I remembered what I had been told about the last tenant.

On Sunday morning, as I lay in bed, a tremendous hammering started somewhere. I was only half awake. The banging seemed to be on the door of the other room on the first landing, the one rented by the unknown people with whom I shared the gas stove. Another shower of blows made my lampshade vibrate. I could hear the door shuddering and the lock rattling. Then I heard the janitor shout: "Come on out, d'you hear? How many are there of you? Who's in there? I know what's going on! Open this bloody door—I don't want no more nonsense from you, I've had enough of it!" Then the hammering began again, followed by another bout of yelling. It went on for about ten minutes, until I heard the bolt slide back, the door creak open, and a child's voice whispering inaudibly.

And by Monday morning the room was vacant. Later that day, on one of my journeys to the gas meter, I looked for Mrs. Lawton. The happenings upstairs had left a peculiar air of tension in the house, and I thought she could explain them.

I found her in her apron, sour and tight-lipped, sitting wearily on the kitchen steps in the November sun. When I asked her what all the commotion was about she only shrugged her shoulders.

"Bloody people," she said contemptuously. "There's always somebody causing trouble in this house. I'm sick of it. They knew we don't allow kids here."

Apparently a couple had taken the room about a fortnight ago, then a few days later had smuggled in their two children. Four of them were living in a room no larger than mine. There was only the one double bed. Then the parents began arriving home in the early hours of the morning, shutting the front door each time with such a crash that it woke everyone in the house. Mr. Lawton suffered most. He was on the first floor, sleeping over the door, and each time it happened it nearly jolted him out of bed. He warned them repeatedly about that, she told me. This particular Sunday they had been out all night somewhere. No one knew where they went. Only the children were in the room. I thought of them crouching behind the bolted door, terrified, with all that hammering and shouting paralysing them with terror.

### iii

I sat in a café in Deptford High Street. I was beginning to look round vaguely for some sort of job, but the weather was bad, and I had taken refuge in this place. It was really a dairy, smelling of milk, with marble-topped tables and rough chairs in front of the counter.

Sitting there, day-dreaming, I let a sad luxurious feeling flood slowly into me, as I thought of the solitary nature of my life. Then for a brief moment I felt a chill gust of fear, believing I was still caught in loneliness, forgetting about Jessie. But I had found someone, and my lips smiled, for I was watching the past ebb away, vanquished. A real life seemed to have begun for me, imperfect, yet full of promise and hope, and I thought of an existence like an unfoldment, where joys and troubles sang hoarsely, all together, from a single throat; until I almost leapt to my feet. Life was a poem. It sang like a brook, endlessly, bending in the sun. And now I was fully awake.

I found myself sitting near an old man who was wearing the filthiest raincoat I had ever seen. It was tied with pieces of string at the wrists to keep out the wind. The hairy claw-like hands which jutted out were massive. They looked capable of crushing rocks back into dust. Suddenly this man addressed the room in a thunderous voice.

"Lady!" he said.

People were watching him from the corners of their eyes. His face reminded me a little of my grandfather's, though his moustache was more extravagant, gushing down over his mouth. His hair, coarse grey with a red-rust glint in it, was like a mane, and in fact his heavy head bore a striking resemblance to Maxim Gorki's. I looked at his torpid fist, as slow as another world, and imagined the horn on his palms. I even found an old envelope and tried to make a rough sketch of him as slyly as I could, arranging my left arm on the table as a sort of fence in front of me.

Everyone seemed determined not to be contaminated by this tough old vagrant. The newcomers gave him a quick look of displeasure and sat down farther away, as if to keep out of range of his fleas. In his deep rumbling voice he was trying to draw our attention to a large black cat asleep on the empty chair beside him. Then he ignored the human company and addressed his remarks to the animal. He seemed utterly engrossed in it. I looked at his huge frame and tried to decipher the rumbling that came from inside him, like hollow noises from deep in a cavern. At last I understood. It was the same thing repeated over and over.

"You know, don't yer," he was saying.

He leaned forward with his great dirty hands outstretched, dragging the chair and cat farther under the table, away from the draught of the door. Outside the wind and rain had become a gale, driving straight down the street. Through the shop window I saw people walking half bent, half turned, trying to avoid being lashed by the force of the storm. It was like watching a silent battle: people were struggling, leaning and pushing, and the street swiftly clearing.

The old man sat up and leaned back in his chair. He roared out again, this time distinctly: "Another cup o' tea, lady—when you ain't busy." The woman gave a curt nod in his direction and continued to serve her more respectable customers.

He sat there with great patriarchal dignity. I admired him without understanding why. He made me long to see my grandfather again. Then he saw me watching him and his yellow serene eyes flickered with amusement.

The waitress stalked up and pushed the tea under his nose without a word. He nodded slowly and pulled out a tobacco tin that was polished with age. From this tin he produced a shilling.

The wind had slackened, the rain innocently pricking the puddles, so I got up to go. When I left, the old man was bent over, talking to the cat once more in his subdued rumbling voice, dwarfing everybody with his enormous back. I almost tripped over a bundle he had left in the doorway.

# Nine

### i

I made my room as decent as possible, and on my first Saturday there, before going to meet Jessie, I glanced round at it anxiously. It was still bleak and dreary, nothing would alter that. But now there were sketches, sent from home, which I had pinned up to cover the walls, and on the dressing-table, in a little blue vase, was a bunch of anemones. I wondered what else I could do; then gave up in disgust. Something anonymous and wretched, connected with the passing in and out of successive tenants, had steeped everything in its solution and made it squalid. There was no defeating that. It was like the linoleum in the hall with its pattern rubbed off, worn to a colourless blur by all the indifferent feet. It triumphed over everything.

At the station, when I saw her step down from the carriage and stride eagerly towards me, swinging a small bag, my doubts and fears dropped away. There was something pale and tense about her face, as she drew closer, that made me uneasy. Yet when she spoke her voice was excited and happy.

"Hallo," she cried. "Guess what I've got here!"

We were walking along hand in hand.

"In the bag, d'you mean?"

"Yes, a surprise. Guess what."

I laughed gently at her; she was so full of her secret.

"I give up," I said.

She stopped among the taxis to show me, under the high glass roof of the station entrance.

"Things for your room," she explained, and uncovered the contents of the bag, one thing after the other, so that I could glimpse them. "A gay bedspread, a red-and-white check table-cloth, and a bowl for fruit. There—aren't I good to you?"

"Very good," I said. "I wonder why."

"Don't ask me," she laughed merrily. "I must be mad."

She hugged my arm as we walked along, then took my hand, giving it a sudden squeeze. A tenderness came into my eyes and throat and I could not speak. I wanted to take her somewhere, to my room, but I had decided to wait until the evening. I was ashamed of it in the daylight, and the time was only one o'clock.

We rattled towards Oxford Street in the tube, and she asked about the room. I told her how drab it was, and about the colour of the walls.

"O dear," she said ruefully, "is it that bad?"

"Worse," I said. "You wait and see."

"I don't believe it. Where are we going now?"

"I'm not sure," I confessed, and she looked at me in mock astonishment, shooting up her eyebrows.

"Are you hungry?" I asked her.

"A little, I think. How about you—how d'you go on for meals now? Do you cook for yourself?"

"Sort of," I said evasively.

"What did you have for breakfast this morning?" she persisted.

"Nothing, really. I couldn't be bothered."

"Good heavens—let's find somewhere, then. Why don't you take more care of yourself?" she cried. I was touched by the concern in her voice.

We went into a small restaurant in Oxford Street. It was crowded.

"Tell me what you've been doing," she said, as she sat opposite me. "Any paintings, yet, for me to inspect?"

"Only this," I said, and showed her the sketch of the old man I had done on the back of the envelope.

"Oh!" she said in surprise. "Who is he? What a strong face—but he's an ugly piece of work. Ugly but attractive—is that what you meant him to be?"

"I suppose so," I said awkwardly. How difficult it is to talk about such things, I thought. "It's not really a success."

"I like it," she said firmly. "Eat your dinner, young man. Anything else to show me?"

"No, only me," I grinned at her.

"Then what have you been up to for a whole week, in a room all to yourself? Aren't you mysterious!"

"I've been looking for a job. I went after one in Deptford, where they wanted a warehouseman, but they didn't think I'd be strong enough. They wanted somebody to lift tiled fireplaces about—that sort of thing."

"Oh no, that wouldn't be suitable for you. I'm glad you didn't get it. Couldn't you get a job at your trade—wouldn't that be better?"

"I could do, easily, but I hate factories. It's like being in prison."

"Yes, I know. How about a clerk? Would you take to that, d'you think?"

"God knows," I said, pulling a face. "I'm a queer fish. And what do I know about clerical work?"

Jessie sniffed her amusement. "If you can write your name you can be a clerk," she said. "It isn't as though you're not intelligent." And she widened her eyes, bending forward across the table. "Have my job in Brum," she offered grandly. "I'm sick of offices, and the boss gets on my nerves—you'd adore my job! Last August the manager called me in to his little glass-walled pen to speak about a very delicate matter. Those were his words, Nick—and what d'you think it was?"

"Go on," I said.

"I wasn't wearing stockings he said, and he hoped I wouldn't be offended, but it was a rule that stockings must be worn. Only I *was* wearing them—some very thin ones! I felt like lifting my skirt up and saying 'Yah!'"

Laughing, we got up to go.

"Now what?" she asked, turning to me.

"Well, we could go to the Monument, and climb up, and then come back by river to Westminster Bridge."

"Can we do that?" she cried. "You mean by boat?"

"Yes, if you want," I said casually, proud of my superior knowledge of London.

"I'd love to!" she said.

Once more we entered a tube station, descending a long draughty slope which streamed with people, and stepped into a train almost immediately to be whisked to the City.

We wandered through the deserted streets between large, blind buildings, towards Billingsgate.

"What a smell," said Jessie, as we drew nearer.

"It's not these offices," I said, grinning. "It's coming from the fish market."

We entered a square, and I pointed at the tall column of stone, poking out of the refuse and stench of fish into the murky sky. It looked ludicrous in its isolation, like something left there by mistake.

"Is that the Monument?" Jessie asked incredulously, as we walked up to the scored base of it. She had expected something grander altogether.

When we came out at the top, dazed by the violent rush of light, she was afraid. A powerful wind pulled at us, and she shrank back from the parapet with a little shudder.

"It's like falling through space," she said. "I'm sorry, but I've always been hopeless at heights. I should have remembered."

Apart from us there was only a middle-aged couple standing close together in silence, looking in the same direction like one person, and perfectly still there at the dirty rim of stone, as though the vast fuming spread of London had petrified them.

ii

We arrived at Greenwich just as it was getting dark. I hurried Jessie along the narrow pavement in the fog-laden street, smelling soot in the fog. The street lamps loomed out at regular intervals like vague yellowish fruits.

"Here we are," I said, halting on the pavement outside the house.

"Why, it's quite large," she exclaimed. It did look rather big and impressive from the outside. But it was like a decayed tooth.

I opened the front door very quietly and shepherded her into the shabby hall, praying that Mr. Lawton would not hear us and come out. Women friends were probably not allowed. His kitchen door opened on to the hall at the end. It was slightly ajar but there was no sound from there. At the top of the house somewhere a radio was wailing out dance music.

From the landing I reached into my room and switched on the light, before standing back for her to pass in.

"Look at your sketches!" was the first thing she said, darting glances everywhere in keen approval. "And what lovely anemones. Why, it's much better than I expected. After all, you're on your own, and you can do what you want now, without interference from awful landladies, once you're in. I think you could be very snug here."

"Let me take your coat," I said, thinking only of time slipping away, the hours being eaten up with words, squandered in conversations. Soon we would have to go back to the station.

Jessie looked at me with calm bright eyes. My hands trembled slightly as I helped her remove her coat. Beneath she wore a transparent little blouse, tinted by her flesh at the shoulders.

"Isn't it strange, having somewhere to go?" she said softly. "Isn't it nice?"

"We're usually wandering about like lost souls," I laughed.

"We are, aren't we? I can't get used to it, not yet."

"I'll make some tea," I said. I had left everything ready. "Sit down and get accustomed to things while I fill up the kettle."

I went downstairs. There was no one about. Most of the tenants went out on Saturday night.

When I came back into the room she was perched on the bed, facing me.

"It won't be long," I said. It gave me an intense pleasure, waiting on her.

"Sit down yourself for a minute," she said. "I like to look at you."

A strange silence fell between us, full of desire. Her face softened with love as she let her eyes dwell on me, and a warm, grateful feeling ran into my heart.

I went out on the landing again to make the tea, and returned to find Jessie pouring milk and putting sugar in the thick white cups.

"You needn't have done that," I said.

"It's automatic," she smiled. "I've been a wife, you know."

"Cecil told me something about it, not very much."

"Did he?" she said startled. For an instant her eyes were hard and acute, over her tea-cup. "I didn't know that."

"Hardly anything. All I know is that his name was Victor—Victor——"

"Massarella," she said, and added with a touch of pride or affection, "He was half Italian. You remember those little figures I showed you, at Cecil's meeting? He taught me how to do them."

"Oh, he was an artist," I said involuntarily.

"In a way. He was at a loose end, like you. He didn't know what he wanted. He was waiting for circumstances to decide for him. That sounds very nice, but it's no good to live with." She gave me a sharp look and ended, "I don't like poverty."

"And that made you come back to England?"

"No, not just that. It was a combination of things. I didn't mind the poverty at first, or the waiting to decide what he wanted—but it turned out that he didn't know exactly *who* he wanted, either. There was another woman over there, that he hadn't mentioned. I don't suppose it was all his fault; I probably drove him to it. I'm hell to live with. Marriage doesn't seem to suit me. It brings out my worst qualities—or perhaps it's my real self coming out then. God knows."

Her mouth was hardened by an interior, past bitterness that was incomprehensible to me. It burned into her talk. I had wished I had not pursued the subject now. Her face had gone unseeing and abstract, chilling to look upon. Then she changed, holding out her cup for more tea, smiling across.

"You remind me of him a good deal," she said gently. "He was narrow and long-legged, too, and he had your dark looks."

"That's it," I said, half seriously. "You've made me a substitute for him."

A twinge of pain went across her face. "What nonsense!" she said, almost in anger. "Don't say such a silly thing."

"Why not," I said quickly. I wanted to soften my wild remark. "I'm jealous of him."

She looked up again suddenly, her face warm, showing her pleasure.

"Are you?" she murmured, putting down her cup.

"Hopelessly," I laughed in relief. "I'm jealous of all the time he spent with you, when I think of my miserable few hours."

She gave her low, excited laugh. "When are you going to kiss me?" she asked softly.

I got up and went over to her, sitting by her side on the bed. We sat there mutely, then she took my hand and pressed it, turning up her face to me. She sat very still, her feet not quite touching the floor, waiting for me to kiss her. Her wistfulness had gone now, and her eyes were strange and heavy. There was something naked and yearning in her face, taking possession of it, making it shameless and animal. The change was startling. Desire fumed up into my mind, darkening it, as I looked at her.

I took her in both arms, silently, and she pressed her small head like a hard ball against my chest. Still I did not kiss her. She was stroking my hand.

Then I was kissing her face and ears and throat, touching her hair. She kept lifting her head up with a faint cry to avoid my mouth. All around us bloomed a deep silence. It had formed itself into a cup to hold the tiniest sounds.

"Turn off the light," she begged, as she unfastened her blouse.

Her body flowed away under my hands like silk. I touched her breasts, almost in veneration, and they grew big and heavy, round and fat, like full moons. Her belly, a full vessel overflowing silkily, quivered between us as she pulled me to her. I tried to make myself light, so as not to crush her, but she was spreading herself under me like a mattress, pulling my full weight down upon herself, as if the humbling discomfort gave her added pleasure.

Yet she did not become humble, but grander, until her womanhood seemed to fill the room with all the archaic richness of life. And instead of shaming my tense skinny body, she ripened it with her presence, which I knew was something immense and magnificently generous, sun-like; not just for me. It waited for every man.

I pressed my face into her belly, and felt its flesh spilling past my mouth, a warm silky tenderness, running into the dark hollow of her lap. I could hear her voice murmuring and crooning softly above my head, and I hardly recognised it, for it had taken on this same quality of silkiness. Then I sank into deafness, within my hot desire.

It was my first act of love. In her wild spasmodic passion Jessie dug her fingers into my sides, so that I almost cried out, hearing her own involuntary final cry, before she relaxed and went slack, weeping hysterically, quite brokenly, for a moment. For me it was as if all the accumulated bitterness of my body had poured away, like poison released from an aching, malevolent place, leaving me calm and free of pain, full of wonder and gratitude. We lay in the darkness, still as stones, as though buried in black earth.

She was peaceful now, and seemed very far away, the strange wheel of her desire moving her off. Then she came back, as it revolved once more. I felt her give a start of fear as someone tramped heavily and loudly up the stairs towards us.

"It's all right," I whispered. "I've locked the door."

Someone else began to climb up. Now it was delicious to listen to the footfalls coming nearer and louder, then dying away. They passed only a few feet from where we lay, naked and white as peeled wood.

"I shall miss my train," she said suddenly. "Oh, Nick, I shall have to go."

She asked me not to turn on the light until she had dressed. When I switched on, the callous blaze of electricity was a shock. We both winced, squinting ruefully at each other and rubbing our eyes.

"Don't look for a minute, please," she pleaded. "Turn the other way." She was peering into the rickety mirror above the dressing table, powdering her face.

Then she had gone quiet, combing her hair.

"What a freak. Oh God, what a mess," she said in disgust.

I stood behind her and put my arms round her waist.

"Shall I miss my train?" she asked pathetically, speaking to my image in the mirror.

"Does it matter?" I asked.

"There's my mother, Nick. She worries so."

"I don't care," I said. "I don't want you to go."

She touched my hand, smiling.

"But I must," she said.

"Will you marry me? Can't we be married?"

She started, exactly as she had done when someone came up the stairs, and turned to face me, the comb poised in the air.

"Don't ask me that, please," she said with great bitterness, out of a white face.

The words fell in a shower, cruel pointed drops, scalding me.

"Don't ask . . . ?"

She did not answer, but tugged bitterly at her hair, combing.

"I want you . . . don't you understand?" I said dully, in a hollow voice.

She tried to pull away. "I can't, Nick. Not again," she said stonily. "Why talk about it? Be happy with me like this."

"Happy?" I sneered, lost in misery.

"Yes, happy. There'll be other times . . ."

"No!" I shouted in frenzy.

Quivering, I let her go, and we left the room and descended the stairs in silence.

"We must hurry," she said, as we came out in the street. She hesitated, a little ahead, not sure of her direction, and as she turned her head I felt a spasm of hate for her, and for life. I could not understand what had happened to ruin everything, when we had been so happy. It seemed like a blasphemy.

I glanced at her face as we sat in the tube train, swaying towards Euston. It had altered terribly, as though something had stripped it, bared it to the nerves, and I looked at her in despair, blaming myself for this whitened, bared look. In London I often saw such faces, as if the people were victims, pitifully turning this way and that, torn by unseen stresses that they should never have been called upon to bear. Had I helped to make Jessie like these others?

But I wanted her. Nothing else mattered. To let her go now was impossible, like a mutilation.

We reached the station fifteen minutes too late. Her train had gone out on time. There was nothing for it but to wait in the great dismal hall, or go into the streets again.

"You'll be so late," I said. "It's my fault, isn't it?"

"What shall we do now?" she asked, in a strangely calm voice.

"Perhaps there's a café open somewhere."

Hope tumbled back into me. I could not help rejoicing because of my short reprieve.

It began to drizzle as we left the station. We searched street after street, but everywhere was closed. It was nearly midnight.

I drew her into a doorway, unable to bear the tension between us.

"Jessie, I want you, I want you . . ." In the taut, dropping silence my voice was a hoarse whisper, and I hardly knew what I said. I kissed her throat, pressing my lips against her soft flesh, unable to speak. She shivered, stroking my head gently. Then she held me away and looked into my face with large sombre eyes.

"Do you?" she said helplessly. "Are you sure?"

We stood in a deserted square some distance from Euston. Now, as I watched, her expression changed with a weird slowness, as though a mask was being peeled from her face, and a look of horror came into her eyes. She was staring over my shoulder, and when I turned I nearly cried out myself in terror. At my elbow a man stood swaying on his feet, blood streaming down his face. Under the street lamp, the empty space of the square behind him, he looked hideous. A drizzling rain soaked down on his head and shoulders.

"Call . . . an ambulance," he mumbled. "They . . . they . . . beat me up." He did not fall, but stood straddled with closed eyes. I snatched Jessie's hand and ran with her to the phone box. My hands shook as I made the call. Then we fled from that nightmare scene, back to the station. My fists were clenched, my face stiff with disgust. I felt cursed with ugliness, and hated all men, all life. The whole city seemed an unclean, repulsive place. I shrank away from the contagion of things.

At last, after nearly three hours, the train to the north was ready to leave the windy, early-morning platform. At the door of one of the dripping coaches Jessie faced me and grasped my hand, gripping it in a firm handclasp like a man.

"It's all right, darling," she said. "Goodbye for a little while . . . till next time."

"I want to come with you." I felt numbed and withered.

"Stay here," she said. She stood in the corridor, leaning out.

"Come back," I said wretchedly. "Come back and marry me."

"I'll come back," she said in a dazed voice. "I want to. Yes, I'll come."

## iii

She came several times, but she would not marry me.

"Oh, don't ask me," she said fiercely. "It wouldn't be any good. It wouldn't be fair to either of us. You'd hate me after a few months, and I should be disappointed in you, perhaps. Isn't it better like this, as lovers? Besides, I've had my fill of marriage. Once bitten, twice shy."

There was a pause. The memory of the man she had left in America made her voice shake, when she tried to go on.

"Marry me," I pleaded in a yearning voice. I no longer cared how I humiliated myself.

She shook her head sadly. The obstinacy in her face and figure suddenly goaded me.

"Then leave me," I shouted, choking with fury. "Go away. Why do you come here, if you don't want me?"

She put her hands quickly to her face, as though warding off a blow, and the tears came. She sat on the bed, on the brown hairy blanket, her shoulders shaking. It was the first time I had attacked her. I stared helplessly at her stricken face, and standing there all my passion drained away, leaving me cold and empty.

"I can't go," she said at last, in a suppressed, strangled voice. "I can't leave you, I don't know why. I wish I could."

Gradually I came to understand that the part of her that was deeply hurt, when she had lived with Victor, was afraid of exposing itself to more injury. So she held back. In my letters I kept prising away with words, stubbornly, with all the selfishness of love. I wanted her. I knew the strength of my hunger and tenderness; and she had only been waiting for someone to really need her.

"You haven't even got a job," she said. It was her last refuge: she was about to give in.

"I'll get one," I said grimly.

One Wednesday in December I packed my suitcase, pressed down the cheap tin locks, and left for Woodfield. I went straight home and told my mother I had come back to get married.

"Oh yes," she said. "When is it to be?"

"I'm serious," I told her.

"I should hope so!"

I floundered before her contempt. "That's that, then," I said.

"Don't talk so daft," she said. And her eyes clouded with tears. "Oh Nick, how will you live?"

Her voice wrenched at my heart. I turned from her, afraid, because she was so near in the blood. She understood me through and through.

I was glad to see them all again. My sister Irene was becoming a tall, wispy girl, her mouth thinned by timidity, not attractive. And the old man seemed still as strong as ever, still lively; he had not lost any of his curiosity and greediness for life. He was beginning to be more of a fixture, to sit longer in the house, reading Edgar Wallace and watching everything over his spectacles which were bound round on the bridge with black cotton. Though he was undeniably part of the household, people were apt to overlook him, like a piece of furniture they ceased to notice. And this gave him an advantage. He sat apart in his corner looking slightly sardonic about the head, stiff and grizzled, encased in deafness and old age. He had seen too much to stir himself now. He let others worry and get themselves excited. Nobody was concerned about him because it was obvious he was not unhappy.

After a few weeks I found a job in an insurance office in New Street. I felt less of a prisoner in a strange job which had no connection with my trade. It seemed temporary and different, and not the turning-back in my tracks which I dreaded.

In Birmingham I went to the registrar's office, and a fortnight later we were married. The problem of a home was solved for the time being, when Jessie's mother offered to have us in the top two rooms of her house. It was a raw, ochre-coloured place, fairly new, stuck on a hillside about four miles from the city centre. It had an arbitrary look. The remnants of a village straggled around it, crumbling old walls and damp cottages which were being replaced by square brazen bungalows, thrown in from the edge of a suburb.

Mrs. Hammond was a widow and a semi-invalid. She had moved from the village to the bigger, isolated house, and remembered the time when the tramlines were extended and a terminus created at the end of her little street below, linking it to the centre of the city. That was the end of village life. But an open country-side stretched out beyond; I thought I would enjoy living there for a while, even though Mrs. Hammond did not approve of me. She was prepared to do all she could to make us comfortable, but she thought Jessie had brought disgrace on her: first of all with the divorce, and now this affair. She was a curt grey-haired York-shirewoman, looking out bleakly from her little hoard of insults and tribulations. Her own husband had left her years ago. Then he died, and I imagined her grim satisfaction. She looked on me as one more misfortune, and accepted me stoically, with a wintry smile of distaste.

From the beginning she was very kind. But there was an underlying silent hostility always present. She spoke in a quiet, exhausted voice, giving her daughter sidelong, vindictive looks. It made me flinch at first, when I had to face her alone and talk to her. Her icy smile unnerved me. It was a delicate situation. And I understood perfectly well why she resented me, and was ready to pounce bitingly on Jessie. I had a dubious background and an even more doubtful future. But slowly the atmosphere relaxed, and I got the measure of her. We were all forced to adjust our-selves and make allowances, in order to live together.

In her good moods Jessie seemed to almost relish the atmos-phere of tension. It seemed to amuse her.

"How she hates you!" she chuckled one day, when we were alone in the house.

"Is that funny, according to you?" I asked, on my high horse.

"I think so," she laughed.

iv

We were given our own brass key to the front door. One eve-ning, as I stood slipping it in the lock and glancing sideways down the hill, I had the strange feeling that I was repeating a character-istic action of my father's; that he had gone through these very movements hundreds of times, glancing sideways just as I did. Yet I could not remember ever seeing him do it. And when Mrs. Frost poked her head out of her door a few yards below, beaming up at me, I called "Good evening" exactly as I knew my father would have done. I even detected in my voice that same bright, nervous note which was the eagerness to please, so characteristic of him. It made me wonder how alike we really were.

When we visited Woodfield at Christmas I seemed to sense a change in him. I noticed it most of all in his attitude towards me. If he still regarded me as a hot-headed young fool, bridling and arrogant, then he had come to accept me as one. But I doubted if he saw me in that light now. I was with Jessie, married, and therefore a potential family man. So a good many things were changed.

I wondered if the change had taken place mostly in myself. Certainly I was more tolerant now, and felt I understood my father better than ever before. There was no desire to fight against him; those days of anger and revolt were done with. For the first time in years I felt a real sympathy stirring in me, as I watched him making those familiar gestures of the shy man, when he greeted us on Christmas Eve. He was casual and restrained, and if I had been a stranger I would have thought him indifferent. But he had the northerner's distrust of words, and the queer, gruff shyness of the workman, the man who uses his hands. He was friendly but unruffled, showing no surprise, as though I brought home a wife every bank holiday and he found it rather monotonous. I was grateful because he did not fuss over us, and a pang of love or admiration went through me. I saw how full of quietness he was.

Later, when he began telling us in a serene voice about all his jobs, the hardships and misfortunes of his life, stretching his long legs before the hearth, I liked him more than ever. He sat there in his navy-blue suit that was rubbed shiny at the seat and elbows, speaking very quietly, out of a nostalgia of his own. When I looked at my mother she was dreamy-eyed, drinking in each word. He spoke out of a simple dignity, his grey eyes shrewd with humour, and I remember glancing at Jessie's face, suddenly proud that she should hear the story of this independent, unbeaten spirit. But she gave me an unmistakable look which said, 'Like father, like son. What have I let myself in for?'

My mother was smiling gravely, shaking her head.

"Sometimes I just don't know how we managed," she said. "Many's the time I've gone without food to feed *him*," and she pointed half-humorously at me, making a rueful face. "But the worst time was when we lived in those awful rooms, in that condemned house in Castle Bromwich, and you worked at that rubber-tyre factory for thirty shillings a week, during the slump—remember?"

She had turned to my father impulsively, her face flushed with so much reminiscence.

"Remember!" he exclaimed, looking up in wonder. "I'll say I remember."

"What a terrible place it was," she marvelled. "All those rats! They were a real nightmare to me. I never knew where one was going to jump out from." She dwelt on it all luxuriously, relapsing into silence. Memories flushed over her face as she sat there. "Remember those rats?" she asked him.

He laughed.

"I'll never forget that rat I found in my shoe once," he said. "I nearly jumped out of my skin when it squealed—I'd put my foot on it!"

And my mother gasped in appreciation, shuddering her shoulders.

"What a house that was," she said.

v

With the short Christmas break behind me I was back at the office, clattering up and down the long slopes on the tram again, morning and evening.

When I arrived home on New Year's Eve Jessie told me in one breath that her mother had gone to bed with a sick headache and that we were both invited next door, to drink a toast to the New Year.

I let out an exaggerated groan. I wanted to paint, and I hoarded all my free hours like a miser now. Also I was hopeless at small talk.

"You go," I said. "I don't want to sit there and make conversation. Tell them I can't drink, it makes me dizzy. It's the truth, anyway. I'm intoxicated enough without wine."

"Very funny," Jessie said. "You know they'll be offended if I go by myself. We shan't be there long, and after all it's only this once."

I knew I should give in, but made a show of independence.

"Why should I want to drink to the New Year? How do I know I'm going to like it? I may hate the sight of it."

"Oh, don't be silly, they're only trying to be friendly. Eat your dinner, it's getting cold."

Jessie decided to dress up for the occasion. She put on a thin woollen dress with a wide green belt, then dashed back to the bedroom for earrings and a coral necklace. I refused to do anything, though I needed a shave.

'Next door' was a bungalow about twenty yards away. We stood shivering in the night frost, knocking at the door. Then we went in.

We hardly knew the young couple who had invited us. But they were determined to be warm and friendly; it was the season of goodwill. For the rest of the year they would probably nod vaguely in our direction; but now they were set on entertaining us.

"Please don't stand on ceremony, either of you," cried the young woman. "Call me Jane, not Mrs. Franklin. And this is Dick. What will you have to drink?"

Her husband was a fair, courteous fellow. He drifted politely about the room as if he wanted to efface himself. At the right moments we found him hovering at our elbows to attend to us.

"Care to try these pastries?" he murmured. "Or some cake?"

"Do have something else," called Jane, from her seat near the radio.

They were both kind persons. I sat primly, struggling to force my speech down the normal channels. Then Jane snapped on the radio, and a sentimental voice ran into the room, low and musical, with sugary intonation, recalling the events of the past twenty years.

"Switch that off, darling," said Dick, in his gentle voice. "They don't want to hear that, surely." He was being manly and considerate.

Little by little we became less stiff, more informal, though still very guarded and polite. A syrupy, nostalgic note crept into the conversation, similar to the radio programme, and somehow

Jane began talking about the end of the war in Europe, and her experiences. She had been a telephonist at some fire station in the heart of London. And as she described the mad scenes, when she was unable to resume duty because the streets were so jammed with people, I asked myself automatically what I had been doing on that same Victory Night. Yet I did not have to think. It was enough to focus my memory on what happened then.

I remembered it vividly. It was two years after we moved from the old district. The whole street was out for the celebration, dancing and singing and getting drunk. I was alone in the house. I sat grimly in the living-room with taut nerves, reading a book, perhaps with a foreboding of what was to come. Unable to absorb the sentences, I gave myself principles and reasons for sitting there, instead of joining in with the others. The din outside sounded false and loutish and mongrel-like, but that was not my real reason. I always avoided communal activities.

Hearing a faint sound, I looked up to see the inner door opening. Then a young marine and his girl entered the room. I gazed at them in a kind of dazed expectation, at the youth's pink scoured face above the rough cloth of his uniform; yet they were both total strangers. As I looked I thought how natural this was, on such a night. The very air was seething and electric.

"Hallo there!" the marine said, exactly as if I were an old friend and he had caught sight of me in the street.

I sat transfixed, although I was not surprised. It was like watching a nightmare. Then I felt a shock of rage, as the intruder shut the door carefully behind him and lounged there, his hand on the doorknob.

He was grinning broadly, though a little bashfully at first, throughout the whole incident. But the slim, dark-haired girl had a worried look. She cast anxious glances at her companion, who seemed to have enough confidence for them both. For him the commotion outside was sufficient justification for anything.

I sat still, holding my book.

"What about coming out, old man?" the marine asked, and his grin widened. "Why not join in the fun, eh? Come on, be a sport. Nobody's indoors tonight."

"Sorry," I said in a cold voice, "I'm reading." Under my

assumed nonchalance I was bristling with hate. My remark made him tighten his face and lose some friendliness. Then his manner of speech changed abruptly, as he tried a different approach.

"Aw, come on, brother. Not that important, is it? This is something special, you know. Isn't it, Joyce? You don't want to sit here reading, not tonight, surely! What is it, anyway—political?"

This stupid question enraged me. I supposed he was referring to the forthcoming General Election.

"It's a book," I snapped. "It's got print on the pages. I'm reading it, or I was. Do I have to fill in a questionnaire? You go along, I should. Join in the fun and don't worry about me. It's very nice of you, but I'm anti-social, I'm afraid. I shouldn't enjoy it, believe me. I'm only being selfish by refusing."

It was my first attempt at a sarcastic speech, and in my anger I had got it out without faltering. The youth laughed uncomfortably, glancing at his girl. He meant to exchange an arch look with her, but she did not respond. She seemed unhappy. The marine was not so sensitive. He was slowly becoming more baffled and annoyed. My outburst had nettled him.

"Come to please us, then," he said, lounging and grinning mechanically, "and make the party bigger. How about that?"

It had got beyond a joke, and he was beginning to appear a fool in front of his girl. His eyes went sharp with irritation above his grin.

"Well, what about it, chum?" he grinned with constraint.

"No thanks," I said coldly. "I'd rather not."

I could feel myself trying to sink down, to rivet myself to the chair, in opposition. Nothing would make me move.

"Why though?" asked the marine, and swung round to his girl again, as though nonplussed. "I don't get you. What's the objection?"

"Don't you want to consider me?" I countered. "I was enjoying myself, reading this novel, till you came in. I didn't ask you to come. Why not let me go on enjoying myself?"

My opponent came farther into the room. He put one hand on the table and lounged on his other hip.

"What's it about?" he said insolently. "What's so good about it, that you can't put it down?"

The ugliness in his voice, even more than his words, made my hands tremble with rage. The girl stood back near the door in painful silence, as if the scene distressed her. I wanted to give in because I felt sorry for her, but everything had gone too far now.

"Is it exciting stuff?" he repeated.

"You wouldn't think so," I said.

He came forward once more, chuckling ominously, looking backwards at his girl.

"Listen," he smirked playfully, standing directly over me, "if you don't come quietly, we shall have to use other means! Eh, Joyce? We shall have to employ service methods! We're not having anybody indoors in this street tonight—is that clear? You can read another time, can't you? You can do that any night. Not that important, is it? Can wait, can't it?"

He leaned down confidently and grasped my arm.

"Come on, there's a good chap," he said.

I snatched my arm away viciously.

"Stop that!" I shouted. "Hop it!" I was choking with rage, and as I sat there I yelled up into his face. Through the half-open front door came gusts of laughter and singing, and the sounds goaded me further into fury. The marine stepped back in alarm, his face comical with surprise. Yet his mouth was still fixed in its expression of grinning amiability. I knew I was behaving like an idiot, but an intolerable mixture of fear and outrage had taken possession of me. It worked in my blood like poison.

"You fool!" I snarled. Nothing else would come. "You blasted fool!"

I sprang to my feet and stood facing them. The marine had retreated to the door. It was all too much for him.

"All right, keep your shirt on," he was saying, shrugging his shoulders contemptuously as he turned to his girl. He muttered a sarcastic comment that I failed to hear completely. My face was twitching. I kept trying to check the wild storms of emotion whirling about inside me.

"Won't you come ... really?" the girl faltered, smiling painfully, as they paused in the doorway. It was like an apology.

I could only glare speechlessly at them both. When they had gone, and I heard the front door bang, I was at first unspeakably relieved; then a bitter shame spread over me. I never saw them again.

Looking back now, I was inclined to despise those times of extreme seriousness, when I was so raw, so rigid with youth. Besides, it was perhaps dangerous to be like Orpheus and look back; though I felt I was safely out of that underworld.

# Ten

## i

It was the New Year. I sat at the table with Jessie. We had just finished our Sunday breakfast. I stared out at the deceptively bright sky with its nervous hurrying clouds. The intense cold pinched at my fingers, even indoors, giving my nails a bluish tinge. Over our heads I imagined a wind like a piece of clear ice honing the slates.

Mrs. Hammond, dressed in a flowered pinafore, was carrying the used cups and plates into the kitchen, and Jessie leaned across towards me.

"I'm going to have a child," she whispered, her face surprised. Then she sat back and watched me blankly.

The ancient triumphant feeling passed through me at once, the feeling that men nearly always have, regardless of their circumstances, before exterior things overwhelm it. I seemed to know that my eyes were shining.

"Are you pleased or angry?" she asked, almost in fear.

"I don't know," I said. "How do you feel?"

"Awful," she said. "I don't want it."

Then her mother came back into the room and we fell silent.

Slowly the spring came round, and the first blackthorn blossom appeared almost overnight, like a snowfall, scattered along the leafless hedges. Jessie broke off long pieces to arrange in her big green vase, searching patiently until she found them with those angular, dramatic gestures which appealed to her. It made her happy, and for a while she was full of eagerness and hope.

"I want the child now," she said. "I do, I really want it."

Then a bout of depression sent her veering back into doubt. As she grew bigger, she would say:

"I must have been stark raving mad. I don't like children. I don't, Nick. I've always kept clear of babies, they make me feel ridiculous. What are we going to do about this? I tell you I don't feel a scrap of mother-love in me, not a morsel."

Sometimes she looked at me, on the verge of tears, hating me, with a look which said: "Do something!"

Another time she would be curious, almost reverent. Lying in bed she would say suddenly: "Quick—give me your hand. Feel it moving, can you? There!" It was a source of wonder and fear to her.

The word October sounded harsh and insistent now, like a loud bell. In the end we avoided saying it. The month crept nearer, dominating us. We were to ring the district nurse when it was necessary, and later on the doctor would come. Jessie refused to go into a hospital.

October arrived, and the date was passed. Nothing happened. Then on a Saturday the moment descended on us, and the house itself became a hospital. In spite of all our waiting we were caught unawares.

ii

It was six in the morning. Jessie must have slipped out of bed and switched on the light. As I came to my senses I realised that she was standing near the door, calling to me.

"Look!" she whispered, in an awestruck voice. "Oh look, look!"

I lay there, dazed with sleep, blinking up stupidly into the glare.

"Please—wake up!"

There was a lump of thick blood on the floor between her feet. Her nightdress and thighs were smeared with blood. It was on the sheets. She took off her nightdress and stood in her vest, clutching a towel, trying to wipe the mess off her legs. She was whimpering with fright like a child. As I crawled out of bed I struggled to grasp the situation. I wandered up and down the room, mumbling, "Put something on, put some clothes on." It was a sharp frost, and that was all I could think of.

A fresh gout of blood fell on the carpet, and I heard the soft thud.

"Oh!" gasped Jessie.

And this was too much. Terrified, she began to cry. I groaned. "For God's sake get back into bed!"

"I can't, it's all on the sheets—oh! there's some more. What shall I do?"

I went downstairs to fetch her mother. She had heard us and was already dressed. Then I scrambled into my clothes and ran out to phone for the nurse. An icy wind struck under my clothes. There was not even a cat in the street. The day was just breaking, hanging its grim crumpled linen in the sky. I clenched my teeth, unable to stop shivering.

The air in the phone box was stale. I hunted through the soiled directory for the number, but ended up by asking the exchange for it. At last I was through.

"Yes?" said a muffled, sleepy voice. "Hallo?"

"I'm speaking on behalf of my wife, Mrs. Chapman," I said ridiculously. "I think she's started with the baby."

"The pains, d'you mean?"

"Yes—well, no. I don't know about pains."

"Then why d'you think——"

"She told me to tell you," I rushed on desperately, "that a lot of blood's come away." The dubious voice at the other end disintegrated me.

"Oh yes, some blood. Might be a false alarm. Righto, then— tell her not to worry. Is she all right?"

"Yes," I said, not knowing what she meant.

"Very well. Tell her not to worry."

I felt a little sick in the stomach. Climbing back to the hill street I noticed the sodden lumps of autumn leaves at the base of a high wall. I found myself looking about as though my eyes were acting independently, fastening on absurd things. On the way back it occurred to me that I did not even know if the nurse was coming.

My mother-in-law had already taken charge, making Jessie get back into bed and lie still. But there was fear in the house now.

"Are they coming?" Jessie asked at once, as I entered the room. I knew then that she was expecting the doctor as well.

"She didn't say, but I should think so. I told her, and she said, 'Don't worry.'"

"What d'you mean?" she asked wildly. "What did you tell

them—that I was having it?" A spasm crossed her face.

"It's all right, yes, I told them about the blood."

"But didn't you say it was urgent? Oh, you're hopeless! You'll have to go again. Why don't you tell them I'm having it? Tell them to hurry up!"

Her voice was rising to a shriek. Then her expression had gone blank and one hand flew to her mouth, as another pain came.

"Tell them the pains are getting faster," she cried as I turned to go. "Tell them."

When I went out for the second time I saw the blue car approaching the house from the opposite direction. Something had made me look back.

The nurse stayed for a few minutes, then hurried down to her car to go back for the gas-and-air apparatus. Things were more advanced than she had thought. She was a stout, pale woman, with a tight fixed smile. She looked hard and efficient.

In the kitchen Mrs. Hammond was already boiling water, messing about hopelessly with pans and kettles. The strain was beginning to tell on her.

Upstairs I sat on the bed and tried to stroke Jessie's head. I felt utterly helpless.

"It's awful," she groaned. "Oh—it's coming again!"

She kept trying to screw herself into a ball, moaning with a terrible sound that I had never heard before. It seemed to come from the back of her throat, an inhuman, animal moaning. I was frightened. She hardly knew me now. The pain lay between us horribly, and she was buried in it, alone with it. I was useless.

A lull came, like a false calm between two waves. Jessie looked at me with her large frightened eyes.

"Don't stay here," she said quietly, in a strange remote voice. "I think I'm going to scream next time. You don't want to hear me. It's terrible, I just can't help myself. I can hear the scream coming out of my mouth, but I can't stop it."

"I don't care," I muttered, stroking her head hopelessly. Then I saw her eyes go blank, the distorted look running into her face. The lips lifted from her teeth and her body bent again, as if in an attempt to escape this approaching flood of pain.

I knew there was no longer any love between us. Nothing was

as real as this pain. Nothing could be placed against it, nothing as real, as black. Everything was being stripped away, laid bare, or else shrivelled up to ash and clinker by it, burnt up and dropped aside. We were two human creatures on a bed, nameless and wordless, one sitting, one lying down; one with a face of pity and fear, one with ugly distorted features. There were no thoughts, nothing else mattered. We were stripped of everything for which there was no absolute need. We had only our poor bodies, racked or trembling, and our eyes of flesh.

"Go away!" she moaned at me, out of her pain.

At last the nurse came back, tramping solidly up the stairs with her apparatus.

"How are we getting on?" she rapped out. She gave me a quick shrewd look. "You can stay a while if you wish," she said. "You won't be in my way. But if you do, I'll make use of you."

She stooped over Jessie. "D'you want him in the room?"

"Tell him to go away," whispered Jessie.

And the woman straightened up, nodding casually to me. Turning to the bed, she blocked me out with her heavy back.

Downstairs I sat in the living-room, in front of the fire. I picked up a book and dropped it again in distaste. Now and then I heard stifled cries, and the loud matter-of-fact voice of the nurse. I looked at one of my framed water-colours which hung over the mantelpiece. I could not understand why I had done it. It seemed about as necessary as caviare.

In the end I found myself reduced to examining the pattern in the carpet, studying it minutely. And I thought of all the paraphernalia that a man erects round his life, and how sickening and preposterous it was. What was the good of it all, of painting, philosophy, religion? One elemental fact smashed it all to pieces. Where did I get my notions of superiority? The glory of the poet—how did I ever deceive myself with such rubbish? I sat there, stupid and wooden, outwardly impassive, jeering mercilessly at myself. Life seemed a pack of lies.

My mother-in-law kept going to the bottom of the stairs to listen. She stood out in the hall so that I could not see her. She did not want me to see her. I believe she was standing there mutely, wringing her hands.

"I don't know what to do with myself," she kept saying, in a strained voice. She was grey at the lips.

Drawing up a chair before the fire she sat down mechanically with some knitting. As she fumbled with it, gazing into the flames, I could feel waves of hate coming from her.

"Are you upset?" she asked me once, looking at me almost curiously, amazed at my silence. The question brought me to my senses; I was alert at once. It was a form of attack. I bridled at the vindictiveness underneath it. I knew exactly what I was expected to say, but in some perverse way I became more aloof, as if indifferent to the whole affair. I forced my expression to convey this deliberate nonchalance.

"Are you?" she repeated softly. She sat watching me, round-backed, unable to restrain her bitterness.

"Yes, a bit," I said sullenly.

"A bit!"

She said no more. She sat tight-lipped, encased in her hatred for me.

But I refused to be bullied. I would suffer in my own way or not at all. My face felt thin and bleak and hard, like an axe-head. I struggled to keep it expressionless. Then all at once I seemed to see myself. Even at this stage I was clinging to my precious dignity. And I thought in disgust that if I were drowning I would probably insist on doing it in my own individual way. What could be more ridiculous than my attitude? Was it because of a fear of showing emotion? Yet I persisted, almost fanatically making my eyes as hard as flints, taking care not to betray the least flicker of emotion. Then a ghastly idea floated into my head. What if I suddenly burst out laughing in the midst of it all?

Gradually the words and labels which were neatly fastened on things began to blur and soften, slipping out of my mind smoothly, like salt pouring away, until I was left with Life, Evil, Birth, Death, Pain, Fear, Pity, Grief, Joy. These were the last to disappear. In the end I was left with myself. I felt hollow and empty, like a piece of old wood, sitting motionless. At my side Mrs. Hammond stirred her feet, but I did not look at her. I stared into the fire. All my nerves and life had gone into my ears, which were straining for the slightest sound.

I thought: 'Up there she is folding up her legs and screaming, naked and alone.' But the whole house was silent.

My mother-in-law seemed to be bending lower and lower over her knitting, her hands clenched on the grey wool. I hated the way she sat there, as if all the woe of the world bowed her down. She crouched forward, huddled over her woe and loathing for me. It was because of me that her daughter was suffering. How could she help hating me? I did not blame her, but I refused to sit like that. My pride would not let me.

Then a poem started uncoiling in my head, and I snatched up paper and pencil to scribble it down. That must have disgusted her, I told myself afterwards, though she had not spoken, and I seemed to sense a feeling of relief in her. For the tension in the room was slowly sending us mad. And in some strange way a bond was being created between us, despite everything, because we were sharing this experience.

When someone knocked on the front door we both jumped to our feet. It was the neighbour, Mrs. Franklin. She wanted to know if there was anything she could do.

"No, thank you," said my mother-in-law, stiffly polite. She had no wish to be seen by strangers at such a time, I thought, though she was forced into politeness. She was really very reserved.

"Are you sure, quite sure?" the young woman persisted. "Wouldn't you like a cup of tea?"

Mrs. Hammond shook her head. "We'll be glad when it's all over," she said, and could not help adding, "Or I shall."

Mrs. Franklin remarked on the pallor of my face. It was always like that, but I said nothing.

"I should go out for a while, if I were you," she said. "There's nothing you can do here. Why not go up in the garden? I'll tell you when anything happens."

### iii

I walked outside and climbed up to the high garden in bright sun, thankful to escape from the stifling room. It had been a sharp morning frost, but now the sky was as blue as an iris. There was an amazing clarity everywhere around me. I seemed to be noticing every blade of grass, every leaf, every pebble. The colours were pure and brilliant. Everything was sharp and microscopic, like a jewelled pre-Raphaelite painting, except that it stirred and breathed and chattered, the path crunching under my feet.

At the top of the garden the apple trees were like baskets brimming with light. Birds frisked in their branches. I wandered across to the ramshackle wooden shed and took out a spade. I thought I would turn over some weedy ground. It would pass the time. Grasping the chill steel of the handle I struck down blindly into the earth. Facing me, lower on the hill, was the vertical back wall of the house. It was brilliant with sunlight. Jessie lay somewhere behind there. It was like a fantastic dream, watching things happening as they always did. I could hear the milkman dragging his green trolley up the slope, rattling and banging along with a gang of children behind him.

A sudden impulse made me drop the spade and start hurrying down. I pushed open the door and went inside. Mrs. Hammond had not stirred from her chair. She glanced up and smiled forlornly as I entered the room. She was past hatred now, as I was. I believe we felt a little compassion for each other.

Within five minutes I heard the new-born child utter a single cry. It was a beautiful sound. It pierced through my heart and shattered it, then cemented it anew, all in a flash, washing it in fresh blood, whole and clean. That was how it felt. It took less than a second. The heart stopped dead, then began to beat cleanly again, singing its song of triumph.

Then the nurse came tramping down, flushed and triumphant. She even laughed gaily at us as she shouted in her news.

"A boy," she shouted. "Perfect, no trouble. No need for Doctor."

She started clearing away, bustling up with jugs and pans of hot water. She seemed to enjoy making as much noise as possible. Each time she descended she brought an enamel pail which was full to the brim with blood and slimy slops and water. I carried it outside and poured the contents down the lavatory. Back she came after a few minutes with another full pail. I took out three or four bucketfuls of this diluted offal, walking in and out, until I thought that there could not have been much more if they had disembowelled her. But I was not really startled, not seriously. I was too dazed and entranced at the thought of my son. My head was filled with its magnetic little cry.

The nurse came in importantly with the placenta. It was wrapped in brown paper, and she told me to put it at the back of the fire like a log. Jessie described it to me afterwards as looking like a piece of raw meat, dripping with blood. The nurse held it up casually for her to see, her arm shiny to the elbow.

There was much coming and going. The tidying-up went on for an interminable length of time. We were not allowed up until she had made Jessie 'pretty'. It went on and on until we were sick of it, and my mother-in-law flickered her eyes at me, shrugging her shoulders sardonically.

At last I was allowed to see her. After such a time I was over-whelmed by the importance of the event. Feeling ridiculous I pushed open the door, went across the bedroom and sat down by the bed, before I managed to raise my head. Jessie was sitting up, her hair neatly combed and a blue woollen jacket around her shoulders. I was shocked because she looked so white, as though drained of all her blood.

"Very pretty," I said gently, and laughed.

The nurse held up the new child, a tiny red, crumpled crea-ture, gasping for breath in her hands. She swaddled it and placed it in the cot, then went away.

We were waiting to be left alone. Jessie managed to smile feebly, but it was not a success. We sat there, very wan, like dif-ferent persons. Yet not as strangers, for we remembered our old relationship. When she spoke it was plain how frail it had made her. I could see that she was badly shaken. And it was clear that something fundamental had changed between us.

We did not take much notice of the child at first. It seemed hardly alive, when I peered in at it; just a motionless bundle, tiny, and dreadfully helpless. The cot swallowed it up.

We sat quietly in the afternoon silence of the house, saying very little. I noticed that Jessie's eyes were still full of fear. And for the rest of the day she remained afraid, living almost wholly in her memory of it, like a nightmare she was unable to shake off. I felt as though I had hardly any emotion left, as though it had been crushed out of my body violently, like breath, by a pair of huge hands.

"Use this lovely pain!" the nurse had told her. "Don't waste it! Press!"

Once she got Jessie out of bed and walked her round the room supporting her, to speed up the process. Jessie had nothing but praise for the powerful nurse, but the pain still haunted her.

"It was awful," she said repeatedly, in a low voice. "You haven't any idea." She gave me a strange, fearful look, as if I intended to hurt her.

That same evening I sat at the table, copying out the poem I had scribbled during the morning. Then I went upstairs and gave it to her. She felt too weak to sit up, but she took the paper from me, holding it silently between her hands.

I stood by the bed, feeling foolish, waiting for her to finish reading. It was a poem about birth, about the mystery and wonder and terror of it, and at the same time it was a love poem. I wanted to thank her in such a way that it would somehow lessen this gulf which had opened between us. That was why I had given it to her now. But it would serve me right if she laughed, I thought. I had chosen a bad moment; perhaps the worst possible one.

For answer she raised her delicate face to me. It was all lit mysteriously by a warm luminous joy within her. It glowed there among the sheets like a candle nestling in snow.

iv

At first she was disappointed with her baby because it seemed so impersonal; just a helpless, crying thing waiting to be fed. She had to keep reminding herself that it was hers.

Then one evening I came in to find her happy. Her baby was beginning to know her. It smiled. Frowned. Another flickering smile, comical, came and went. "He's smiling at me!"

"Might be a bit of wind," I said.

"I don't think so. Look—again!"

And after a few weeks she said:

"I catch myself looking at this child with the silly drooling look I've seen on other mothers' faces. Would you believe it—I never thought I should end up like that!"

Quickly the spring drew near again. I almost feared it, the life bursting out in the warm weather, the hedges strewn with blossom. The thought of it made my job tighten round me like a vice. I became conscious of my nature squirming in a steel grip.

We would have angry little discussions. They rose up sudden as squalls. It was always the same argument, the one subject.

"Can't you settle down, now you've got me?" Jessie asked. "Doesn't that make a difference?"

"Jobs are jobs," I said.

"Other men aren't restless, are they?"

"How do I know?" I laughed.

"Of course not. They're not."

"They are, but they're broken in, resigned to things," I said.

"What you mean is they've got a sense of responsibility. Why can't you be like them?"

"You know why," I said.

"Do what you want, then," she cried. "Oh, I hate these moods of yours. You make me feel guilty, as if I've trapped you. What do you want to do, really?"

"I don't know. Paint, I suppose. Write poetry."

"But there's no money in that!"

"Exactly."

"Yet you wanted to marry, and you must have known what it would be," she said bitterly. "How did you expect us to live?"

There was no answer to that.

One Sunday morning in late February the weather seemed full of approaching spring. I looked out through the window at the shimmering blue sky, vibrating like a great icy bubble. Later, when the sun shone full into our room, bringing the paintings alive on the walls, I could not stay indoors. I went out for a short walk.

My body felt horribly puny and ill-treated, winter-bitten, until it slowly adjusted itself to this sparkling new world. The weak sun warmed my face, touching me softly, face and neck and hands, with ineffable sweetness. As I walked on, the insanity of my office work, waiting for me on Monday, became something

I had proved monstrous and impossible in my very blood. And I had solved nothing by my marriage. I was as restless as ever. My inner and outer life were just as incompatible as before.

Back in the house, I thought again of the old vagrant I had tried to sketch in the Deptford café, and spoke to Jessie about him.

"I wonder where he is now," I said.

She looked at me warningly, knowing that when I spoke of tramps I was kicking against the pricks. She was about to bath the baby. As she darted about the room, spreading newspaper on the table, then getting a towel, she said over her shoulder:

"You and your tramps. Just because he needed a wash you thought he looked romantic. Get me the soap, will you, and that bit of flannel in the tin basin."

"He didn't need a wash," I said. "That's where you're wrong. He was one of the original Norse gods, in human form. Probably he'd been mending his iron cooking pot, the one he uses for a hat when it rains." I had been reading Carlyle. "If you came across Vulcan, would you expect him to have a clean face?" I added, not realising I was in the wrong mythology.

Jessie snorted in disgust as she poured the water and tested its heat with her elbow. "I expect he worked on a coal lorry, or at the gasworks."

"I tell you he was a tramp. If he turns up around here I'll bring him home for a meal, to prove it."

"You do," she said, "and you'll do the cooking between you, for I shan't do it."

But she was not listening. I was looking at my son, so tender in the bud, with such a delicate flushing of pink all over, softly mantling his skin. I loved to see him naked. He sat in the water, only half liking it, upright in the enamel bowl. What a compact, tiny head he had, perfectly formed, and as I watched it trembled, wobbling, like a nut on its stalk, the eyes wonderingly bright, roaming the room. He was half afraid, yet he liked it. When the water ran over his shoulders, sluicing down his front, he opened his mouth, and both his arms quivered slightly.

"You little mite!" cried his mother, beaming with pride as she always did, forgetting about me. I took up my drawing-book and tried to sketch him. I had tried before, and failed each time, not realising what a terribly difficult thing I was attempting. This time I attacked my paper boldly, darting down quick, nervous strokes without bothering about accuracy, and had more success. I managed to dash off three sketches before he was dressed. They pleased me. Then I laughed. The child was more alive than any drawing.

When I carried him out to the pram a happiness rose up involuntarily, swaying inside my chest. Carrying the child was like holding a future, hugging it to me. And a great richness ran into my body, down my arms.

Jessie was clearing away when I returned. From the seriousness of her face I guessed that she was about to make a speech.

"You read things into people that aren't there," she said suddenly. "I don't see anything remarkable about tramps. They're failures that's all. D'you mean to say you'd like to be dirty like that, and never wash?"

"Who said I wanted to be one?" I said. "You always make it a personal matter." And knowing it would irritate her, I added, "There's a vagabond, an Arab, in every man somewhere. Now and then he gets the itch to wander, this Arab, and pops to the surface. Women are different."

"Well, don't let me stop you. You're free to go any time as far as I'm concerned. Please yourself. Wander as far as you like, but don't expect to find me waiting for you when you get back."

"Why can't we both wander?" It became a ritual; I knew the answer before I even asked the question, but I still waited hopefully.

"What about the baby? And jobs, and money? You're ridiculous, you're not practical."

"Then let's be ridiculous for a change."

"Air this napkin and stop chattering."

But I kept returning in my mind to the huge man in the café whose moustache was like my grandfather's, and whose features resembled Maxim Gorki's. He chimed in me symbolically whenever the sense of confinement grew too strong. I still had the sketch on the old envelope somewhere.

Looking out once more at the pure glittering weather I thought of how the sky waited, day after day, always blue as a

flower behind its veil of clouds. It was like the other world which
I felt was blooming softly all around me, a magnificent new existence. But I could not break through to it. It beckoned me like a
springtime.

"Why can't you be content, like other men?" asked Jessie.

I made no reply. How could I tell her that I wanted more life,
when I had so much already? How could I explain what I only half
understood myself?

v

In this same February, while the baby was four months old,
my grandfather met with a street accident in the centre of Birmingham and was taken to hospital. He was knocked down and
crushed by the rear wheel of a bus. Usually he would not venture
out of Woodfield now, but on this Saturday night he had done.
He was crossing the Bull Ring, an open cobbled space set on a
steep slope. His deafness was always a danger to him in traffic;
and this long cleared space was a sort of marshalling point for the
ponderous red double-deck buses. They halted and manœuvred
here, in front of the blackened church, crushing the fruit stones
and apple cores which littered the cobbles on market days, before
sliding away down the sloping streets. And on Saturday all the
vegetable and fruit carts would be drawn up in the gutter along
one side, outside Woolworths, hemming in the traffic. A slowly
reversing bus had knocked him down.

I was not told how serious his accident was. If my mother
knew she kept it from me. Even after I had been with her to the
hospital I did not know.

When we arrived at his bed he was dozing. His expression was
exactly as I had seen it hundreds of times, when he used to fall
asleep in his chair at home. We sat by the bed for ten minutes.
My mother was fidgeting anxiously. She asked me, whispering in
my ear, if I thought she should touch his shoulder, because our
time was nearly gone. Then I saw his eyes flicker open. He was
watching us. It was a strange moment. He looked without speaking, like an animal. I nudged my mother but she had noticed. She
forced her face into a smile.

All at once he tried to drag himself into a sitting position, clutching the sides of the bed and gasping. My mother cried out in alarm and jumped up.

"Don't be a fool!" she hissed down at him.

He struggled again, and she turned to me in despair. "What shall I do?" she asked tearfully. "He'll make himself worse."

Suddenly she leaned at the old man in a flash of anger. "If you don't lie still, I'll fetch the nurse over," she threatened.

He dropped back, a look of surprise on his damp face. He beckoned to her with his eyes, dumbly, and she bent down to him.

"What is it?" she hissed, not able to shout in the silent ward. "What d'you want?" He was watching her mouth shaping the words.

His eyes shifted to me, the inquisitive stare resting on my face without recognition, then swinging back to my mother.

"Tell the little bitch to fetch the bottle," he said suddenly in his loud whisper.

My mother went red with embarrassment and hurried off to find the nurse. The old man closed his eyes, ignoring me. His expression was mild and contented.

Two days later I travelled across Birmingham to the house in Woodfield to ask for news. My mother was away; she had gone again to the hospital, so I sat down to wait. Only my sister was in the house. She moved about the room in silence, thin and bird-like. She was shy of me now because we rarely saw each other, and I tried not to follow her movements. She made me feel old and coarsened.

"I thought you weren't allowed to visit on a Thursday," I said. She had crouched down beside me to get her sewing things from a gaily-coloured straw basket.

"No, you aren't," she said, moving away. "They sent for her."

My heart went down.

"Sent?"

"Well, when she rang up after tea, they said she'd better come."

"You mean he's worse?"

"They wouldn't tell her anything. They just wanted her to come."

"Where's Dad?"

"He's gone as well."

At nine I was still waiting. Then I heard the latch of the front gate. When my mother came in she was carrying a bundle of clothes. I recognised them, but I only stared at them stupidly in vague surprise, not understanding.

My mother looked very tired. She passed through to the kitchen with the clothes, then came back to answer the question in my eyes.

"He's dead," she told me.

## vi

It seemed incredible. But he was no longer about, so I was forced to believe it. Strangely enough, the fact of his death did not sadden me. Somehow it failed to penetrate as a loss. For nearly a week I kept thinking that I should meet him unexpectedly, in a street somewhere. I even looked out for him.

One evening I was telling Jessie about my visit to the hospital, trying to re-create it for her. I had told her before, two or three times. I wanted her to see the old man lying there, so that she would have the scene safe in her memory. I was afraid it would be lost if I did not share it with somebody. Telling her this time I found myself emphasising that he looked so alive, though he had been on his deathbed. As I sat watching him I never dreamt that he was dying.

Then I wandered farther back, remembering bits of my early life, when my grandfather was younger. Not that he seemed younger then, or older at the hospital. He was like a piece of stone that the lapping water of years hardly altered. The changes were imperceptible. In my memory he remained the same.

I told her how I seemed to sense the different, grander world he carried with him, the nineteenth century, with horses in the streets, when he had lived his own youth, and how it all stood over my childhood and enriched it. Snatching up one incident after another, I struggled to bring back the strangeness and mystery, the intense potency of those days.

Yet I felt already that they were ghostly and insubstantial. It was as if the old man had taken the living part of my childhood with him when he died. I heard myself talking, droning on, and it was like listening to the story of another man's first years, instead of my own. Even as I spoke I could feel the shadow, reality slipping away, and my inadequate words settling like dust, covering up the faint traces of those feet, so that I lost my way. Finally I told Jessie that it was no good, that I could not do it. I had lost my childhood in order to gain my manhood.

"Wasn't that how it should be?" I asked her. "We were gluttons to want more," I said perversely, knowing that I contradicted my own feelings. "Why did we feed ourselves on memories? There was something horrible about it, like eating carrion."

"Yet we do," she said slowly. "I wonder why?"

Her voice was distant, as though she spoke out of sleep, and I guessed at once that she was answering me vaguely across her own past, out of the spell it cast over her. I was a little jealous of it.

"Do what?" I said. "Why what?"

"Stop trying to catch me out!" she flashed. "I heard. I know what you mean."

"Better tell me, then," I mocked gently, "because I'm not sure myself."

But she was still resentful.

"You're not the only one with understanding," she said hotly.

"Who said I was?"

"And what cheek you've got!" she went on in a rush. "It's you, you're the dreamy one, not me. Sometimes I have whole conversations with myself, when I'm supposed to be talking to you. You're somewhere else. You can complain!"

I let her go on. She was on a favourite topic now. There was a light bantering note in her voice; she was not really serious, but I held my breath. At any moment she might branch off into anger. So I kept silent. With a woman it was better not to argue: I had learnt that much. It was so easy to touch something else off unwittingly.

We were sitting at the table, having our evening meal. Jessie was frowning slightly with resentment or impatience. How soft she looked in the lace blouse, I thought.

I had my fork half way to my mouth.

"Listen," I said.

For in the air there was a rumour, like a stirring of leaves.

"What is it?" she asked, staring at me. "What can you hear?" And a smile rose on her face, a softness.

Then I laughed. We both did.

"What are we laughing for? Oh, you mad devil!" She was helpless with laughter, looking at my face.

"It's the wind of spring," I said.

She stopped laughing then, because I had spoken seriously.

"Words, words," she scoffed, watching me.

I could almost hear the spring growing closer, heaving itself through the earth. It was drawing nearer and nearer, surging, plunging forward, through a sea of death and darkness. It shattered the silence of winter, cleanly, like a vast shout.

It held out its arms to us.

www.ingramcontent.com/pod-product-compliance
Lightning Source LLC
Chambersburg PA
CBHW011749010726
47498CB00012B/2993